Strike It Lucky

Best Wishes

D. W. Tomlinson

Published by
www.printandpublishbooks.com

First Edition published 2024

Printed and bound in Great Britain by
www.printandpublishbooks.com

A catalogue record for this book
is available from The British Library
ISBN
978-1-915730-94-7

About The Author

It was 1976 when David Tomlinson (son of a coal miner) left his comprehensive school in the coal mining village of Maltby. He was 16 and had secured an apprenticeship with a local fabrication firm. After being unable to obtain oxygen and acetylene his factory closed within 18 months, due to industrial action by the British Oxygen Company, and David found himself on the dole.

After knocking on the door of his local colliery (intending this to be a short-term solution to his predicament) David remained there for the next 35 years.

When his colliery eventually closed in 2013 David found himself once more on the dole and so started his own landscaping business which he ran until his retirement in 2018.

During his retirement David returned to creative writing (an old hobby of his.)

After submitting humorous letters and articles to national magazines (with some success in publication) David returned to a work he started during the 1984 miners' strike.

In his first fictional work “Strike It Lucky” David draws on a lifetime of stories from the community that nurtured him, and skilfully weaves them around a story of great intrigue.

Strike It Lucky

D. W. Tomlinson

Table of Contents

Dedication

With greatest of thanks to Andy Tupholme for loving this story so much.

Without whose help and enthusiasm, I'm sure this work would have remained unread.

Although this is a fictional story some of the characters and events are based on true and... true-ish stories and real people, from various mining communities throughout the Yorkshire coalfields during the 1984-85 miner's strike.

Some names have been changed to protect the stupid.

Strike It Lucky

D. W. Tomlinson

Everyone always said things would get worse before they'd get better. The trouble was no-one said just how bad worse was going to be.
Someone once said: When you've got nothing, you've got nothing to lose. Well, I suppose that's how we saw it at the time.
We were wrong; we had each other.

Prologue

1981

A hubcap rolled down the embankment, ricocheted off a large boulder and came to rest by the crystal-clear water of a small stream. On the road above, a white transit van had escaped the same fate by bouncing off the crash barrier. “For fuck’s sake!” cried one of the two masked men in the back. The driver tore off his balaclava and his passengers regained their balance before making their way to the back of the van. The men peered through the back of the window. “There’s nothing following us, slow down.”

The van moved off, resuming its journey across the Pennines at a slightly less frantic speed.

Over the next couple of years, moss began to form on the discarded hubcap, it was eventually picked up and taken away by a couple of ramblers with a passion for keeping the moors tidy.

Chapter One

Colin's Big Step

It was getting colder. The fine drizzle that had been falling started to turn white as it settled on Colin's jet-black hair. The puddles that he trudged through were beginning to form complex patterns of ice-crystals. The sky thickened with cloud and the woods beneath them darkened.

Colin left the path and jumped from one rock to another, until he reached the far side of a small stream. Colin knew this spot well. As he sat on the embarkment gazing into the ice-cold water, something caught his eye. Just for a split second, he thought he saw something move beneath the water… and there it was again, darting from rock to rock. Of course, sticklebacks! Colin remembered fishing for these as a small boy. Who was it? That's right: he and Timmy Dawson had made a fishing net from a pair of Tim's mother's stockings.

As he stared out at the surrounding woods, he realised they look different somehow. The trees didn't look so tall now. He wondered, was this part of growing up or was it the fact that these particular woods were on the outskirts of a small mining community for which firewood had become a valuable commodity over the past year, as coal to fuel their homes gradually became unavailable.

To his right there was an outcrop of rocks beneath an old oak tree. He remembered the bigger kids making a swing there. They had laughed themselves silly the day the rope had broken sending Timmy's brother Mark, Tony Mulligan and Pete Morrison plummeting into the stream below. They were happy times, but they had been children then, and children know nothing of the real world. Colin used his multi-coloured Genesis on tour t-shirt to wipe away the tears that had begun to well in his eyes.

Getting to his feet, he climbed the rocky outcrop and looked up to the overhanging branches of the oak. He could see a small piece of rope still tied to one of the branches. Water was trickling down its length and dripping from the frayed ends that had broken under the weight of three silly schoolboys all those years ago.

Colin took his own rope from his shoulder and threw the heavily tied noose over one of the oak's thick branches. Retrieving it, he placed the noose around his neck and closed his eyes. He thought once more about those happy days he had spent as a child, then stepped off the rock.

Colin heard a loud crack: the crack of a bone snapping; he had expected this. And there was a splash: he had not expected this. Then he felt a searing pain in his ankle; he had not expected this. He opened his eyes to find himself in a small stream, a length of rope rapidly coiling itself in his lap. Suddenly it stopped, as the end he had neglected to tie off came to rest. The searing pain in his ankle shot through his body. His vision became blurred as it hit his brain. It was at that very moment he could have sworn he saw himself and Timmy Dawson watching from the far bank, a younger version of himself, granted, holding fishing nets and a jam jar, but it definitely wasn't them, was it? Colin reached out his hand and tried to stand, but the pain in his ankle was too great and he completely lost his vision. Finally, Colin passed out.

It was three weeks to Christmas and if the two men who pulled up outside the Miner's Institute that morning had emptied out their pockets, they might have been able to raise enough money to buy a turkey sandwich, although at first glance you might not have thought so. The car they were driving was a 1969 Ford Mustang, purchased approximately one year earlier by its present owner, Numbnuts Harrison, with the intention of renovating it to its former glory. Unfortunately, for Numbnuts the mineworker's union, the NUM, had called a general strike a couple of months after he had bought the car. This meant that anyone who was a member of the NUM (which Numbnuts was) had now been on strike for almost a year. As a result, he had never had the money to carry out the renovations and the car was falling more and more into disrepair. To make matters worse someone, for their own amusement, had scratched the name *Sally* after the word *Mustang* on the rear fender.

This sort of thing seemed to be the norm for Numbnuts; nothing ever seemed to go right for him. Even his nickname, Numbnuts, had been given to him by his so-called friends after he had announced that he and his wife had been trying to have children for the last two years, but to no avail. The only three people who called him Danny, his real name, were his wife, Sandra, his best friend, Lenny Grey and Lenny's wife, Sue. Lenny had grown up with Numbnuts; they had gone to school together, started work at the mine together and even lived across the road from one another. There was no doubt that Lenny was Numbnuts' best friend. And there was no doubt that Numbnuts was a millstone around Lenny's neck. At least that's how it sometimes seemed to Lenny.

Lenny had always had great hopes and big ambitions, and why not. He was only thirty-two. He had been blessed with brains and foresight. Unfortunately, he was also blessed with great human kindness, a sense of loyalty, and Numbnuts!

Lenny knew he was involved in a strike he could not win; one day he would return to work and struggle to pay the bills that had been mounting over the past eight months. He knew the mine would eventually close. He knew he was destined to live and die in a run-down pit village and that nothing exciting was ever going to happen to him. He knew in his heart of hearts that all his dreams were just pipe dreams. What he didn't know was just how wrong he was.

Numbnuts turned off the ignition and Sally, (as he liked to call her) purred to a halt. Lenny and Numbnuts sat quietly waiting for a few moments. Lenny eventually took the unlit cigarette from his mouth.

"Does this cigarette lighter actually work in this thing, Danny?" he asked.

Numbnuts contemplated for a short while then shrugged his shoulders. "Don't know." They sat for a short while longer, then he added "I don't smoke do I?"

Lenny put the unlit cigarette back in his mouth. He leaned forward, pulled the lighter free from the dashboard and tried it on the end of his cig, even though it wasn't glowing.

"Perhaps the engine needs to be running" Numbnuts suggested hopefully.

"Try it," Lenny said, leaning forward again to replace the lighter. Numbnuts turned the ignition key and Sally, who had been left in gear, jumped forward and stalled. Lennys head, which was bent forward as he tried to replace the cigarette lighter shot even farther forward and his nose impacted on the dashboard.

"Jesus!" he screamed, with his hands now cupping his damaged nose (just above the broken cigarette in his mouth).

The next few words that Lenny screamed were unintelligible – although Numbnuts had a good idea what some of them were.

The commotion in the car caught the attention of an elderly passer-by. The old man bent down to tap on the passenger window with the handle of his walking stick. He wasn't being nosy. He knew Sally and her owner very well; he also had a good idea who the passenger would be and was merely going to say "Hello". He could hear Lenny screaming at the top of his voice, something about a clumsy idiot who needed to be more careful. His friendly smile was instantly obliterated by the car door, which hit him square in the face as Lenny angrily threw it open. Lenny emerged from the car tilting his head back and firmly pinching his nose in an attempt to stop the bleeding.

Lenny walked in a circle three times, thumped the top of Sally once, and kicked a nearby wall twice before noticing the old man who was spread-eagled on the floor rubbing his forehead. Numbnuts and Lenny hurriedly helped the old man to his feet. After a violent bout of coughing, he sat down on the wall and put a trembling hand to his forehead. Lenny sat beside him with his hand on his nose. Numbnuts joined them and sat on his hands (he figured this to be his safest recourse).

After a few minutes of silence, broken only by the old man's incessant coughing and wheezing, Numbnuts decided to speak.

"Looks like its going to be a nice day dunt it?"

The old man turned to look at Numbnuts. "Aye, started off well, ant it?" He returned to nursing his wound. Numbnuts pressed on.

"Do you think it'll snow?"

Lenny interjected before the old man could reply. “Do we look like we’re from the fucking Met. office?”

There was something in his tone that told Numbnuts he was not yet forgiven. Lenny tipped his head back again and resumed putting pressure on his nose. “Are you alright, Bill?” he asked in a somewhat nicer tone.

Bill nodded his head. “I’ll live,” he said with a smile and then began another bout of lung collapsing coughs. Lenny and Numbnuts looked at each other over the top of Bill who was bent double spitting out phlegm. Bill sat back up and cleared his throat.

“I’ve been looking for you and young Numbnuts here. I’ve got something for you.”

“Oh yes.” Replied Lenny in a tone that made him sound as though he wasn’t really interested. Numbnuts on the other hand sounded positively excited.

“Really? What?”

Bill smiled. “Pigeons, lad! Three dozen pigeons.

Numbnuts looked a little disappointed. “What would we want with three dozen pigeons?”

“There’s a lot of meat on a pigeon.”

Numbnuts looked puzzled, but Lenny’s interest level seemed to rise dramatically. “Three dozen you say... What’s wrong with them?”

“Nowt’s wrong with them, it’s just, well you know... I can’t get up to allotment as often as I used to, and now our David’s moving away.” A warm smile came over Bill’s face. “Good lad our David.”

“That’s your brother’s lad in’t it?” Lenny asked.

“Sister’s,” Bill corrected. “aye, our David’s been feeding them for me, but with him leaving I’m not going to be able to see to um.” He looked a little sad as he spoke. “I’ll miss that lad.”

The despair that was evident in his voice was beginning to embarass Lenny and Numbnuts. Lenny eventually broke the awkward silence. “Where err... Where is David going exactly?”

Bill heaved out another long cough. “Australia.”

Numbnuts placed a reassuring hand on Bill’s shoulder. “Never mind, it’s not as if it’s the other side of the world you know!”

Bill looked at Numbnuts for a moment and wondered if he was joking. The solemn look on Numbnuts face suggested he wasn't.

"Why is he going to Australia?" Lenny asked. "He's emigrating. He's going to live with his mother, my sister, Betty."

"I don't think I know her, do I?"

"No probably not. She used to live across the way in Brookly," explained Bill.

Lenny frowned. Brookly was a small village about four miles away. Who did he know from Brookly? His brain drew a blank and he eventually had to admit defeat.

"I don't think I know anyone from Brookly."

"No," said Bill with a strange kind of awkwardness. "Bit of a one-horse town. Anyway, she emigrated a couple of years ago." Then he seemed to perk up a little. "She's got a lovely house you know; got its own swimming pool and everything, right out int' country… Well, when I say she has, I mean she will have when she gets married to her new bloke."

"What new bloke?" Lenny asked politely.

"The Australian, with the house in the country with…

Lenny and Numbnuts joined in ...the swimming pool."

"When is she getting married?" inquired Numbnuts.

"The 20th. Or David's flying out there next Wednesday, you know. He's having a week or so to meet his new family and all that. Would've gone myself but the doctor's advised against it." Bill gave a slight cough. "You know, because of the altitude."

"Well," said Lenny. "You'll just have to change your altitude and he might let you go!"

The three men sat on the wall and laughed for a while and somehow the morning seemed a little brighter than it did before. Eventually, Bill rose to his feet, which didn't do his chest much good, and after a long hard cough announced,

"Well, I'd better be off, shop should be open now." He paused for a while; his brain was trying to remind him of something. He had his stick; he had his hat…"Oh yes, do you want them pigeons?"

"Yes, we'll come and get them later," said Lenny. As an after thought he added, "Are you sure? I mean aren't they worth anything? I thought pigeons were worth a bob or two."

Bill nodded. "Can be. A good racer can be worth thousands. Them that I've got are worth about ten bob a brace. Do you know where my loft is?"

Numbnuts sensed that sufficient time had elapsed for his forgiveness.

"It's up ont' allotment. I've seen you up there."

"I'll leave you to it then," said Bill as he turned to leave.

"Aye we'll see you later." Lenny and Numbnuts walked up the steps leading to the Miner's Welfare. Bill coughed his way down the road leading to the tobacconist.

Lenny and Numbnuts stopped momentarily to read a poster attached to the club door. It showed a picture of what appeared to be a cowboy playing a guitar with the works, *Chuck Colorado. International singing sensation.* Then, they entered the lounge, the smallest of the clubs three rooms. It was in this very room five days previously, that Lenny and Numbnuts had managed to talk Mick, the NUM secretary, (who was very drunk at the time) into letting them help pack and distribute this month's food parcels. This wasn't something they were doing out of the goodness of their hearts. This was something they were getting paid £4 by the NUM to do; there were hidden benefits too.

The scheme had been set up two months into the strike and was designed to give aid to striking miners and their families. Spoilt and damaged food and other goods that would not normally make it to the supermarket shelves were donated by local haulage companies. Along with goods paid for with cash donations from other sympathetic unions, these were shared out and distributed at the end of each month. The scheme was very successful, mainly due to the fact that local warehouse staff and lorry drivers, many of whom had friends and family in the coal mining industry, had suddenly become very careless when handling their goods. Although there was plenty of food to go around, each food parcel contained different items, depending on availability. The packers, being men of honour, were there to ensure that each parcel contained goods of roughly the same value, that no parcel was worth more than another and that no other parcel was worth more than their own.

Lenny and Numbnuts entered the lounge, they were warmly welcomed.

"Where the fuck have you two been?" enquired one of the four men who were already hard at work, seemingly packing King Solomon's shopping into a mountain of cardboard boxes.

"Sorry Harry," said Numbnuts, "we were..." "We had a bit of car trouble," interrupted Lenny, throwing Numbnuts a dirty look.

"Well, you're here now, so get your fucking coats off and give fucking Levi and fucking Taffy a hand with that fucking lot. Me and Mick's doing the fucking tinned stuff." (Harry liked to swear a lot). "Should have got some fucker more reliable. Still expect to be fucking paid though, even if half the fucking work's been done." (Harry liked to moan a lot).

Lenny and Numbnuts chose to ignore Harry. They picked up two cardboard boxes from a neatly stacked pile in the corner of the room and joined Taffy and Levi at what seemed to be the grocery section.

The four men now entered into a traditional Yorkshire greeting ritual.

"Taffy...Levi."

"Numbnuts...Lenny."

"Levi..."

The next couple of hours passed quickly and in relative silence, which was only broken by Harry occasionally moaning about some "fucking cheap tack foreign corn-fucking-beef" and such like.

As the lid went on the last cardboard box and Numbnuts and Taffy went to get their coats, Levi suddenly turned to Lenny

"I want a word with you," he said quietly.

This came as quite a shock to Lenny who after all had just spent the best part of two hours working alongside Levi in relative silence. He certainly hoped he hadn't offended him in any way. It wasn't good for anyone's health to offend Levi who was six foot four had a chest that would take the average rambler about twenty minutes to walk across. He really hoped he hadn't offended Levi.

Lenny remembered the last time someone had offended Levi. That's right, it had been back in junior school. Levi had knocked two of the guy's teeth our with a single blow. Lenny really hoped he hadn't offended Levi. Lenny clearly recalled watching the paramedics reviving the guy. What a punch! Lenny really, really hoped he hadn't offended Levi. It was a punch that any ten-year-old boy would have expected to win a fight with, and it had the desired effect too. It was the last time Mr Phillips; the PE teacher had offended Levi. Please God thought Lenny; don't let me have offended Levi. Lenny often passed the old school on his way to the infants' school that his daughter now attended and had frequently witnessed old Mr Phillips refereeing a football match on the adjoining field. Lenny thought about that punch whenever Mr Phillips took out his two front teeth to bow his whistle. Lenny prayed he hadn't offended Levi.

Lenny tried to swallow what seemed to be an apple stuck in his throat. "Why? What's wrong?"

"Nothing's wrong. I just need some advice, that's all."

Lenny looked up at the nicotine-stained ceiling and thanked it. "What about?" he asked, as the colour returned to his cheeks.

Levi was just about to open his mouth to speak when he noticed the approach of Mick and Harry.

"Nothing," he said, and then in a whisper added, "I'll see you later."

Mick laid down a large blue book full of signatures.

"Right lads, just sign this."

Lenny, Levi, Numbnuts and Taffy added their names to the list and was each given a brown envelope containing four £1 coins. Numbnuts emptied the contents of his envelope into his hand.

"Doesn't seem as much, does it?"

"What?" asked Lenny as he counted out his money.

"Pound coins, it doesn't seem as much as pound notes."

The £1 note was at the end of its phasing out period. It had been replaced by a shiny gold coloured £1 coin that wasn't very popular and was very easy to lose.

Don't you want us to deliver the parcels Harry?" asked Numbnuts, as he slipped on his coat.

"Fucking don't. No, we want to make sure they get to where they're supposed to be going."

Harry had gone too far. Lenny lunged towards at him. Levi pushed a table to one side and Numbnuts slipped back out of his coat. Mick, the branch secretary and master of diplomacy, quickly intervened by standing in front of Harry.

"It's alright. It's alright. What he means is we've got all the names and addresses. We've hired a van we'll see to it." He added, "If you could run us these down to the Alamo that would be great help." He placed four parcels on the table.

There was a long silence before Taffy eventually picked one up, stacked it on top of his own and walked out of the door. After a few seconds, Numbnuts followed and then Lenny.

Levi stood and stared at Harry for another minute or so, before he too decided to let the incident drop, and left.

As the door closed behind him, Mick breathed a sigh of relief. Harry gestured towards the door with his head. "Fucking wankers."

Sally was packed and ready to go when Levi emerged from the club. Noticing that Numbnuts and Taffy were in the car and out of earshot, he decided to have his little word with Lenny who was holding the boot open.

"Listen," said Levi in a quiet voice, "I've been offered a job."

Lenny looked confused. "You've got a job?"

"That's just it," Levi seemed anxious, "I haven't. I've been on strike for nine months now and the way things are going I might be on strike for another nine. Only," Levi looked a little embarrassed, "it's a proper job and I need my P45, which means I've got to pack the pit in."

"So, what's your problem?" Lenny asked.

Levi still looked embarrassed. "Well, we're on strike and it's a bit like...well...walking away from a fight, if you know what I mean."

"I see," said Lenny with a reassuring smile. "Listen Levi, you probably don't know this, but its sometimes best to walk away."

Now Levi looked puzzled. "Like you just did in there? "Levi, we can't win this strike. Eventually the pit will close. If you can get out now, then get out." Levi still looked puzzled, but after a while, he nodded his head in agreement.

A few minutes later Sally was tearing down the country lane towards the Alamo. Trees flashed by on both sides. Lenny sat quietly staring out of the window. His mind kept returning to Brookly. He had told himself that he didn't know anyone from Brookly, but that wasn't quite true. There was someone from Brookly. Who was it? It couldn't be someone he knew well. Had he gone to school with anyone from Brookly? He didn't think so. Come on, who was it? Lenny decided to stop thinking about it; perhaps it would come to him later. He turned on the radio.

...development in the miner's strike. The Prime Minister reiterated yesterday there would be no backing down by the Government. Talks are due to be held next week between N.U.M leaders and the Coalboard Chairman, Ian McGregor.

The trial at the Old Bailey of the three men accused in the IRA mainland bombing campaign was adjourned today when Mr Ian Justin-Smith, Q.C, read out a statement on behalf of his clients in which the accused men failed to recognise the court. The three men have petitioned to have their case heard in Ireland...

Lenny turned off the radio and began thinking about Brookly.

"Are we going to the pub later or what?" Taffy asked from the back seat.

This was a question Taffy frequently asked; in fact, the only time he didn't ask if anyone was going to the pub was when he was already at the pub, which was most of the time.

The fact was, that Taffy Own was an alcoholic, although this was not something he would readily admit to. He would tell you he was just a young man having a bit of fun, and that was true to some extent, or it would have been ten years ago. The truth of the matter was, that Taffy's carefree attitude, his freedom from responsibilities and his love for lager had left him a twenty-nine-year-old single man with no family, no plans for the future, no savings, no foot on the property ladder and seemingly, no ambitions. Still, he was happy.

"I, er, I don't think I'm going" answered Numbnuts. "Sandra's...er...well it's one of her fertile days today and she wants to...well...you know. Anyway, I want to go out tonight and I can't afford both."

Taffy turned his attention to Lenny. "What about you? You'll make one won't you Lenny?"

"Actually Taffy, we've got a bit of a job on this afternoon. Do you want in?"

Taffy looked a little hesitant. "We're not going to give him a hand with their Sandra are we?"

"No of course not!" Lenny paused for a while to consider whether Taffy was joking. Taffy's sense of humour was strange at the best of times. "It's just something we might have going for some extra money, and we wondered if you wanted in."

Taffy answered without hesitation "If it's for money, I'm your man. Anything short of murder or rape and it makes a couple of bob, I'm your man. Unless of course you want me to murder someone I don't like, or rape someone I do like, then of course, that's different."

Lenny wondered again about Taffy's sense of humour. "What do you know about pigeons?"

Taffy smiled. "What do you want to know? I'm Welsh, aren't I? We've got fields of the bloody things "

Now Lenny knew Taffy was joking. "Fuck all then."

Taffy shook his head. "Not a fucking thing."

"It dun't really matter, just be up at allotments at two o'clock..."

Lenny was unable to finish his sentence. His whole body was been thrown forwards as Numbnuts hit Sally's brakes. It was then, as his head was wrenched to one side by the car swerving hard to the right, that he noticed what had caused the near fatal accident. Someone had suddenly and quite unexpectedly appeared from the woods that lined the road. Someone, who didn't seem at all concerned that he had almost been run down. Someone wearing a multi-coloured t-shirt, with the words 'Genesis on tour' printed on it. Someone carrying a length of rope and using a branch from an oak tree as a makeshift crutch!

Sally slid to a halt in the middle of the road. Its occupants sat in silence for a few seconds, then suddenly, as if a starting pistol had just gone off, the trip erupted into a frenzy of shouting and swearing. Numbnuts gave three loud blasts of the horn (a little late perhaps but this was normal for him), the car doors were thrown open and its occupants spilled out into the road.

"You stupid little bleeder!"

"What do you think you're playing at?"

"For fucks sake Colin!" "Are you fucking blind?"

Everyone was shouting at once. Colin couldn't think of anything to say, so he hobbled on across the road and disappeared into the woods on the other side. The shouting faded into criticism and complaint.

"What the hell does he think he's playing at? Asked Taffy. "He'll get himself killed if he's not careful."

Numbnuts carefully examined the side of Sally that had clipped a few overhanging branches in the attempt to miss Colin. "If he pulls a stunt like that again, I'll fucking kill him."

Lenny said nothing. Something was bothering him about the whole event. Something he couldn't quite put his finger on, but it was bugging him, and it was bugging him even more than Brookly.

Chapter Two

Bill's Pigeons

The cold morning air was heavy on Jim's chest; the wheelbarrow full of logs was heavy on his arms. The mud was heavy on his boots and his wife Janet was becoming heavy on his ear.

"We can't afford it," he said firmly.

The argument was briefly interrupted by three loud blasts from a car horn in the distance. They carried on along the path, moving a little further out of the woods and a little closer to their home. Janet managed not to mention the subject again for a further three seconds (almost).

"But it's only for the weekend and it's free."

Jim answered her profoundly, "Nothings free in this world."

Janet looked down at the barrow full of logs.

"Except for these logs," he added a little less profoundly.

A few minutes later, Janet, who had fallen behind a little and was now struggling to keep her footing on the slippery path, called after her husband, "I need to pee!"

Jim set down the wheelbarrow. "Can't you wait till we get home?" he said, unable to hide the frustration on his face. As he turned, he was greeted by the look of annoyance on Janet's face and realised, she could not.

He gestured to the long strip of meadow grass, which separated the path from the woods on either side. "Better go then."

As Janet waded through the long grass, bobbed down and completely disappeared, Jim took the opportunity to roll a cigarette. When Janet's warm urine hit the cold morning air, a plume of steam rose steadily and seemed to hang amidst the ears of the meadow grass and occasional thistle. Jim couldn't help feeling a sense of serenity. He took a deep draw on his cig, closed his eyes and took in the silence. He only had a few seconds of the enjoyment before the peace was broken by Janet screaming. “Fucking hell!”

“What’s the matter?” asked Jim, the sly grin on his face suggesting that he already knew. “Nettled your bum?”

“I wish! Straight on mi chuffing flow.”

Jim hadn’t married Janet for her ladylike qualities, but she did make him laugh and he was having a particularly good chuckle as he listened to Janet chuntering away in the grass.

“Ooh, that hurt... chuffing nettle... not rubbing a chuffing dock leaf on it that’s a cert... ow! That hurt!”

Jim’s laughter had just about subsided when he turned his attention away from his wife to discard his cigarette and was startled to see a young man a few feet away. The young man, to Jim’s surprise, was wearing jeans, a t-shirt with the words ‘Genesis on Tour’ on it and a pair of training shoes that were caked in mud. This was unusual in itself for such a cold morning, but what was even more unusual was the fact that the young man was carrying a length of rope and was walking with the aid of a tree branch.

“WHAT YER DOIN’?” shouted Jim. This was designed to startle, but it did not; it hardly had any effect at all. The young man simply stopped walking and slowly raised his head.

“Good morning, Jim,” he mumbled. Jim paused for a while before answering. Something seemed wrong, something seemed very wrong. “Morning Colin. Is everything alright?”

Colin’s answer was interrupted by a voice in the grass. “Hello luvvy.”

Colin looked toward the direction of the voice. He was scanning the tops of the meadow grass carefully, when suddenly a head popped up.

“Morning Mrs. Mulligan,” he said.

Janet beamed a smile at him and promptly disappeared again below the grass line.

Jim repeated his question. “Is everything alright lad?” (Colin, although twenty-one was Jim’s junior by twenty years).

“Yes, yes,” Colin answered abruptly.

Jim looked at Colin for a moment before deciding everything wasn’t all right. “What are you up to at this time in a morning?”

he asked, but this time more casually and in a less inquisitive manner. This seemed to provoke a slightly better response.

Colin shrugged his shoulders. "Just out for a walk."

"What have you done to your ankle?" asked Jim, who was now receiving a look from Colin, a look that would have said to all but the nosiest or most insensitive of people 'please stop asking me questions and respect by privacy.'

"I mean, where's your coat? And what's that fucking rope for?"

Colin didn't answer, he just pushed past Jim and his wheelbarrow and hobbled off into the woods. Janet returned, pulling up her knickers on the way, to find her husband looking puzzled and somewhat offended. She made a final adjustment to her knicker-line.

"What was all that about then?"

Jim was still staring after Colin. "Dunno. Mardy little bleeder! Did you see him push past me?"

"Some people are like that, pig ignorant."

Jim was still looking puzzled. "Wonder what the rope was for."

"Perhaps he's going rabbiting."

It was obvious Jim hadn't married Janet for her brains either. "What's he going to do, bloody lasso one?"

Jim picked up the wheelbarrow and started walking away. Janet struggled after him, once again almost losing her footing. "I don't know do I? Anyway, about this caravan…"

Sally was parked at the pit gates. About twenty feet away was a makeshift hut, with the words 'The Alamo' painted across the door. Lenny, Numbnuts and Taffy were dishing out the food parcel to the four token pickets on duty that day. As they did so they told the story of how they had been nearly killed in an accident caused by young Colin Vine. By the time Lenny, Numbnuts and Taffy had bid farewell to the pickets at the Alamo, a light covering of snow had settled on Sally, making her appear cleaner and in much better condition than she really was. Lenny and Taffy waited patiently as Numbnuts searched his pockets.

Eventually Taffy's patience came to an end. "Come on, I'm bloody freezing here!"

Numbnuts searched his pockets a little faster and with mounting panic. Eventually he stopped.

Lenny looked at him hopefully. "Tell me you haven't lost the keys."

"I haven't lost the keys," said Numbnuts reassuringly. "I think they're in the boot."

Taffy tried the boot; it was locked so he thumped it.

"You must have got a spare set," said Lenny as calmly as he possible could.

Numbnuts shook his head. "No, I was supposed to phone…" He stopped suddenly; it was obvious he had an idea. "The previous owner, he has a set."

"Good," said Taffy optimistically. "Where does he live?"

The smile left Numbnuts face as the word "Detroit" left his lips.

After a few minutes of debate, they decided to do the only thing they could do, and Numbnuts set off up the road to the nearest phone box. Lenny and Taffy waited in the car whose side doors, fortunately, had been left unlocked. Lenny leaned forward to turn on the heater. Realising that this wouldn't work without the ignition being on, and he needed the keys to turn on the ignition, he slumped back into his seat.

"This car is jinxed."

Ten minutes later Numbnuts returned. Twenty minutes after that, a tow truck with the words 'Robin's Breakdown Service' printed along its length, finally arrived. A large man in blue overalls stepped down from its cab. He carried with him a small toolbox with the words 'Robin's Breakdown Service' printed on it. Pinned to his overalls was an official looking badge, which read, 'Robin. Head Mechanic.'

"Are you the silly buggers that's locked your keys in the boot??" he asked in a deep voice that suited his stature.

"Are you Robin?" asked Taffy sarcastically.

Robin ignored him and walked slowly around the car, He seemed to be admiring it. "Well, well, well a Ford Mustang. Haven't seen one of these before."

Numbnuts puffed up with pride at the attention Sally was receiving. "I've been meaning to do her up," he beamed.

"So you should, these things are collector's items you know."

"Excuse me," interrupted Lenny. "D'you have any keys that will fit?"

Robin, who seemed to have forgotten why he was there, looked shocked. "Keys, to fit this? You'll not get keys to fit this."

Lenny looked cold and miserable. "You can't open the boot then?"

"Didn't say that." Robin cheerfully pointed to his badge. "I am a qualified mechanic."

"So you can open the boot then?" asked Numbnuts hopefully and then added, "without damaging it."

Robin walked around the car and examined the boot carefully. "I think so."

"Go on then," said Taffy who was now vigorously rubbing his hands together.

"Ah…well… there is a minimum call out fee of £10 for this type of work. I did tell you this over the phone."

Taffy, Lenny and Numbnuts looked at one another. They had been waiting for this moment. They each begrudgingly took out the brown envelope they had been given earlier for their help with the food parcels and handed them to Robin. He counted the money and smiled as he handed back the change.

"Nice doing business with you," he said as he turned to walk away. Robin was stopped by the weight of Taffy's hand on his shoulder.

"Haven't you forgotten something… the boot?"

"Ah yes," said Robin with another smile. "Nearly forgot. Excuse me." Robin moved Taffy to one side, opened the driver's door and lifted a small lever by the seat, which was clearly labelled *Trunk.* The boot sprang open, and Robin walked off towards his truck.

Several seconds of embarrassing silence passed before anyone spoke, and then Taffy shouted after Robin. "Hey, Robin, your second name?"

Robin stopped. He could hardly make Taffy out from this distance.

"It wouldn't happen to be Bastard, would it?"

(It was an old joke, but it helped cheer Taffy up).

Sally pulled up outside number 22, Nelson Road.

"Right," said Lenny as he crossed the street to his own house. "I'm going to have a bit of dinner. I'll come round for you about two o'clock."

Numbnuts acknowledged Lenny by raising his hand in the air, then setting his food parcel on the floor beside his back doorstep, began rummaging around in his pocket for his keys. Then, to his surprise, the door, the door that he had presumed to be locked, opened. A tall man with jet-black hair and a Mediterranean look to him was just leaving. The man, who was wearing a long white coat and carrying a leather satchel was, to Numbnuts' greater surprise, laughing. This took Numbnuts back somewhat. The man was Georgio, (or George) Numbnuts' milkman and, to Numbnuts' recollection, he never laughed. Georgio turned, noticed Numbnuts and stopped laughing. A solemn and almost sheepish look came over Georgio's face. This was the Georgio that Numbnuts knew.

"Afternoon Mr. Harrison," said Georgio in his usual sheepish manner.

"Afternoon."

The two men stood for a moment, as if both waiting for the other to speak. After a few seconds, it became obvious that neither one was going to say anything. Georgio buttoned up his coat and walked off up the garden path. Numbnuts picked up the food parcel and walked into his kitchen.

Sandra was sitting at the kitchen table in her dressing gown. She looked up and smiled. "Hello love, you're early."

"Yes," said Numbnuts as he laid the heavy box on the worktop. "Mick and Harry offered to do the deliveries. What was he doing here? It's not his collection day, is it?" he added as he began to unpack the groceries.

Sandra hardly looked up from whatever it was she was reading. "No, he dropped us a calendar off," she said, sliding next year's calendar across the table.

Numbnuts was finishing putting the food away when Sandra disappeared into the front room.

"I don't really like him, you know," he announced. There was no answer. Numbnuts turned and noted Sandra's absence. "I don't like him," he repeated, this time a little louder.

"Who?"

"That Georgio."

"He's aw wite," said Sandra with a strange speech impediment that she had suddenly acquired.

Numbnuts closed the cupboard door and sat at the table. Sandra returned sucking a thermometer.

"What's wrong wiv him?" she asked.

"I don't know... he's too quiet. He doesn't sa much."

"He guz t' me."

Sandra removed the thermometer and regained her speech. "Thirty-seven point five," she smiled at her husband. "Come on Chuck...and lock the door."

Numbnuts lay in bed thinking. The curtains were closed, but enough light passed through them to slightly illuminate the room.

"I've been thinking," he said in a quiet and almost sad voice. "Perhaps, when the strike's over, we should think of...well...adopting." Sandra didn't answer, so he pressed on, "I mean... I know my sperm count's ok." Then, so as not to apportion blame added, "and so is yours, but it's been a long time now and... well, it's obvious something's going wrong somewhere."

Sandra took his hand. "I've told you before, I don't want someone else's baby, I want my own."

"Our own," correct Numbnuts.

"Yes, that's what I said...our own."

The bedroom fell silent again for a few more minutes before Numbnuts broached the subject again.

"I mean, I feel like I'm letting you down. You want a baby so much... you're so desperate and I don't mind if..."

It was a subject he had long been trying to find the right moment to approach and he desperately wanted to continue, but, to his dismay, he was interrupted by a knock at the door.

"That'll be Lenny."

Numbnuts rose to his feet and pulled on his trousers. "I'll see you later. I've got to go; me and Lenny's got some business on."

As Numbnuts reached the bedroom door, his wife called after him, "Danny, I do want a baby, but I'm not desperate. Don't worry."

Numbnuts smiled and nodded. "Do you want me to put the kettle on, on my way out?"

"No, I'm going to stand on my head a bit longer, let gravity do its work."

A minute later Numbnuts was walking up his garden path to Lenny who was waiting by the car.

"I'll drive," said Lenny.

Numbnuts threw him the keys. As always, he took it as a compliment that Lenny wanted to get behind Sally's wheel.

As Numbnuts went to open the passenger door something caught his attention; there seemed to be a commotion in the alley. He listened a little harder. The commotion in the alley was getting louder. Numbnuts looked at Lenny. Lenny looked at Numbnuts. The commotion was coming their way. Then, without warning, a small boy, approximately twelve-years old, came tearing towards them. In pursuit a gang of about fifteen boys of a similar age.

Lenny grabbed the first boy by the arm and pushed him up against the car. Then he and Numbnuts grabbed the first two assailants by the scruff of their necks. The gang came to a halt.

"What's going off here then?" asked Lenny. There was no answer. "I said, what's going off?"

The tallest of the three boys (Nicky Ryan) pulled at Lenny's arm in a vain attempt to break free, but Lenny's grip remained firm.

"Its him; he shot our cat."

"Did not," said the smaller boy in defiance as he leant back against the car.

"Hey, mind the car," interjected Numbnuts.

The young lad looked at Sally. "Call that a car!"

Numbnuts looked offended but remained calm.

"He did so," called a voice from the gang. "He's got a catty in his pocket!"

"Have not," said the boy.

"Have so," came another voice.

"Liar!"

"Thar' a fuckin' liar!"

"Thar' biggest fuckin' liar ont' estate!"

And so, the commotion erupted once again. As the shouting subsided, Lenny found himself shouting louder than anyone.

"Shut it! Shut it and you," he said pointing at one of the gang, "mind your fucking language. In fact," said Lenny, looking closely into the boy's face, "don't I know your father?"

"If you do," came a voice from about ten yards away, "you ought to tell his mam who it is."

Lenny looked up and realised the gang's prey had slipped away in the confusion. "Come here," shouted Numbnuts aggressively. "We haven't done with you."

The boy raised two fingers then ran a little further down the street before stopping and turning.

"I've seen better cars int' scrapyard. There's more rust on it than you've got on your head."

Numbnuts had to think for a while before realising the boy had been referring to his hair, which although it had been a bright red colour at birth, thankfully had faded to a rusty blonde during his teens.

Numbnuts released the two boys he had been holding. They stood looking up at him quite confused. He gestured with his head. For a moment, the boys looked even more confused, then the penny dropped and the chase was back on.

The drive up to the allotments was uneventful, although the sighting of Levi Jones talking to Janet Mulligan at the bus stop on the corner of Columbus Road was a little unusual. Not that it was unusual to see Levi talking to Janet; Levi knew Janet quite well. Nor was it unusual to see Janet talking to Levi; Janet talked to everyone in the village, whether they wanted to or not. But it was unusual to see Levi wearing a suit and tie.

"Hey, what's up with him?" asked Numbnuts as they passed.

"What's up with who?" said Lenny, taking his eyes off the road for a moment.

"Levi. Look, he's got a suit and tie on."

"Dunno. Perhaps he's going to a funeral."

"Oh yeah." Numbnuts grin deserted him as he sat back in his seat. "Never thought of that."

Numbnuts sat quietly and let his mind wander from the subject of funerals until it eventually settled on the subject of Bill's pigeons.

"I've been thinking. If old Bill can't look after his pigeons anymore, why have us kill them? Why doesn't he just let them go?"

Lenny looked puzzled. "Because Danny," he said as if he was about to embark on a lengthy and detailed explanation. "THEY'RE FUCKING PIGEONS!"

The back door to number 28 Nelson Road opened and a voice rang out from the kitchen. "Hello luvvy, are you in?"

"I'm in the room Janet," replied Sue as she lent forwards to turn down the TV. "Put kettle on while you're in there."

Janet ignored the request and entered the front room carrying two bags of shopping, which she set down on one of the dining chairs. "Here I've got something to tell you, budge up" .Sue moved a little further along the two-seater settee and allowed Janet to sit down. Have you heard about Colin?"

"Colin who?" asked Sue inquisitively.

"Young Colin, ooh what's his chuffin name...Vine. He's only gone and tried to top his fucking self.

"He 'ant."

"He has. Liz Fisher's lads saw him down in woods with a rope round his neck, and I know it must be true. Me and our Jim saw him in woods this morning. He was acting kind of funny come to think of it, and he was carrying a length of rope."

Sue looked genuinely concerned. "Poor lad. Do you know, I thought he'd been looking down in the dumps lately."

"Well," said Janet knowingly, "did you know his girlfriend's been seeing somebody else"

"She 'ant."

"She has. That tall lad that races greyhounds... works at Tesco's. You know him...spotty faced fucker."

"Oh yes, Gary... or Graham... something, works being meat counter."

"That's him. Well, apparently, he's been slipping her some meat of his own for a bit now."

Sue tutted. "Poor lad, is he alright then?"

"According to Liz Fisher, he's broken his ankle."

"Broke his ankle... that's strange."

Janet nodded her head in agreement. "That's what I thought. Normally I'd take that with a pinch of salt, but he was limping when I saw him. Anyway, you never know with Liz; you know what a gossip she is."

Both women nodded in agreement.

"Ooh," said Janet jumping up from her seat, "I was going to put kettle on, wasn't I?" She disappeared into the kitchen. "I've just seen your Lenny. Tea or coffee?"

"Coffee please. Yes, he's popped out somewhere with Danny."

"Yes. I thought it was Numbnuts that was with him."

Sue picked up a large red garment and a sewing box from beside her. "You shouldn't call him that, it's not nice."

Janet reappeared smoking a cigarette. "What? Numbnuts? Every bugger calls him Numbnuts. He dunt mind. Where's your flick dish?"

Sue looked up from her sewing and scanned the room. "It's over there, on the table."

"Hey, you'll never guess what I did today," said Janet with a childish grin. "Budge up. I only went and nettled mi chuffin' flow."

"Silly bugger! How did you manage that?"

Janet drew on her cigarette. "I got caught short in the woods this morning and... Anyway, I ended up sitting on a thistle." She took another draw of her cigarette. "Marvellous," she said with sadness in her voice. "First prick I've had between my legs for six months and it's a chuffin thistle!"

"What do you mean, first prick in six months? Do you mean you haven't...?"

"Not for six months. It's him, he dunt seem interested anymore. I've been trying to talk him into going away for the weekend to mi mam's van. You know, spice things up a bit." The sadness in her voice had now turned to despair. "I don't know Sue; he hasn't always been like that. I used to think that when we buried him, we'd have trouble nailing coffin lid down." Janet projected her forearm and fist from her lap to imitate a large erect penis. "You know."

Sue nodded.

"Anyway, he's off t' boil, and a girl misses that sort of thing." Janet leant forward and held Sue's hand for comfort before continuing, "I don't think he fancies me anymore."

"Of course he does," said Sue with a comforting smile. "Perhaps it's just something medical."

Janet shook her head. "It's not that; I've been to see Dr Greg."

"And what did he say?"

"Well, he said he would like to check him for diabetes, but given the circumstances, you know all the pressure he's under what with the strike and all that... well anyway, he thinks its psycho...sim...psycho...stam...actic." She gave up on the attempt to remember Dr Greg's exact medical diagnosis. "I don't know, he says he's a fuckin' psycho anyway!"

Sue squeezed Janet's hand and gave a reassuring smile.

"Oh Sue," Janet said with a sigh. "What am I going to do? I still love him you know."

Sue gave another smile as she stood up to answer the kettle, which was beginning to whistle in the kitchen. "I know you do, and he still loves you too, don't forget that."

Sue disappeared into the kitchen. Janet picked up the red garment that Sue had placed in her lap but didn't really look at it. Her mind was elsewhere.

"So, what's wrong with the fat bastard then?" she said raising her voice slightly. Sue returned carrying two cups of piping hot coffee, which she placed on the coasters beside the sofa. "Well, it's like the doctor said, it's all up here." Sue pointed to her head. "But there's people who can help, places you can go for people with, you know, difficulties." It was obvious Sue was trying to pick her words carefully. "You know, marital difficulties."

Sue took a sip of her coffee. Janet thought for a while before asking nervously. "What exactly do you mean?"

"Well… I know, for instance, that there's a self help group, for people with… marital problems, up the Edward Dunn Centre."

"I thought that was for mothers-to-be."

"It is. That's on Wednesdays, but there are other groups use it too. That's where I went when I stopped smoking. That's on a Monday," added Sue firmly as Janet lit another cigarette. "The one you want is on a Thursday… or is it a Friday?"

Janet drew on her cigarette and considered Sue's suggestion. "I couldn't. Well… I could. I don't give a bugger me, it's our Jim. He wun't even talk to doctor about it."

"You go then," said Sue enthusiastically.

Janet almost choked on her coffee as she laughed out loud. "ME? On my own?"

"Why not? It might do you some good, you know, hearing people with similar problems. They might be able to give you some advice."

"I'll think about it," said Janet in a not-on-your-Nelly kind of way. She finished her coffee and rose to her feet. "It's better than my other option though."

"What's that?"

"Offer me body to spotty Gary from meat counter." Janet laughed out loud as she picked up her shopping.

"Here," said Sue with a proud grin, "before you go, what do you think of this?"

With that, Sue rolled out the large red garment on the sofa.

"Father Christmas!" exclaimed Janet. "What are you doing with a Father Christmas costume?"

"I've made it for Lenny. He's going to be Santa at our Lisa's school party."

"Bless him. How did you get him to agree to that?"

"Oh, he hasn't agreed to it. In fact, he doesn't even know about it yet."

Janet smiled and shook her head as she set off for the back door. "I'd love to see his face. See you later Sue."

The back door clicked shut. Sue folded up the costume neatly and placed it on the back of the sofa then picked up her coffee cup and turned the sound back up on the TV.

Mainland bombing campaign. The men accused of being members of the IRA had sought to have their case heard in Ireland after failing to recognise a British court. A decision is expected later today.

Taffy kicked the snow from his boots then lazily folded his arms and rested them on top of the allotment gate (which he had now finished kicking). Of course, there wasn't much to look at this time of year. Had it been summer, he would have expected to see half a dozen or more people harvesting carrots and cabbages and such like, but over the last few weeks, Mother Nature had taken in her bat and ball. This, naturally, meant that no one would be playing in the allotment until the following spring. Except for the odd goat and half a dozen chickens milling about in their pens, or the occasional pigeon perched on top of their various lofts, the whole forty acres seemed barren and deserted. Sally purred to a halt and a few minutes later Lenny, Taffy and Numbnuts were standing outside a large blue pigeon loft.

"Here we are then," exclaimed Numbnuts.

"Here we are what then?" asked Taffy. "And more importantly, here we are why then?"

Lenny could tell by Taffy's demeanour that he was a little drunk, but this was expected and so he thought nothing more of it. He opened a large black holdall he had been carrying.

"Sure this is the right place, Danny?" he asked as he produced a tennis racket, a poker and a cricket stump, which he then handed out.

"Yes, I've seen Bill here before."

"Right then," said Lenny as he practised his tennis shot. "In answer to your question Taffy me old mate, pigeon pie!" With that, he headed up the steps leading to the loft's door, pulled out the wooden pin on the latch and then went inside.

After the carnage was over, Taffy discovered an old kettle on the shelf in the corner, along with some teabags, powdered milk and an old mug with a picture of a pigeon on it and decided he deserved a cup of tea. Lenny was studying an unfished crossword in an old newspaper whilst Numbnuts was picking up dead pigeons and putting them into a black bin liner.

"What's on at club tonight?" asked Taffy as he searched around for a spoon.

Numbnuts thought for a moment, "Chuck Colorado."

"Who?"

"Chuck Colorado," repeated Numbnuts. "I think he's a Country and Western singer."

Taffy found a spoon and stirred his tea. "What time are you going in?"

"Depends what time Sandra's ready."

"I thought Sandra was always ready," said Taffy with a wry smile. "What time you going in Lenny?"

"Dunno if I am," answered Lenny, taking a pen from his pocket and setting about finishing the crossword. "She's decided Saturday's *our* night."

"Ha," said Taffy mockingly. "Listen to you; you're both under the bloody thumb. That's why I never got married."

"Lenny looked up from his crossword, "Really? I thought it was because you're an ugly twat!"

"Ha, but don't forget, beauty is only skin deep."

"You must have fuckin' thick skin then."

The violent flapping of a wounded pigeon Numbnuts had tried to pick up, momentarily interrupted the conversation.

"What women really want," added Taffy as he picked up Lenny's Tennis racket and walked over to the wounded bird, "is a kind, caring, considerate man, you know, with feelings." With that, he bludgeoned the pigeon to death. "You see, I know what makes women tick. I'm just biding my time until the right one comes along, that's all."

"And," asked Numbnuts, "how will you know when the right one does come along?" Taffy thought for a moment. "By the size of her bank balance!"

"Or the size of her tits," added Numbnuts sarcastically.

Lenny looked up in amazement. "You really are a dreamer, aren't you, Taffy?"

"We have to, don't we?" said Taffy a little more seriously. "What else is there for people like us? We all know the pit's going to shut and we're going to end up three middle-aged nobodies on the scrap heap, along with three-million other nobodies. So, fuck it!"

Taffy slumped back into his chair. "What's yours?"

"What's my what?"

"What's your dream?"

Lenny was taken back by such a personal question. He had dreams, but they were his dreams. He decided to dismiss the question. "I don't know; never thought about it."

"I know what mine is," said Numbnuts in a soft voice. "I'd like a son; a girl would be alright, but a son would be better. I could teach him to play football, take him fishing… I'd like a son."

There was an awkward silence for a few seconds, until Taffy decided to lighten up the conversation. "I want a pub," he said with a smile. "That's why I want a bird with a big bank balance… so we can buy a pub."

"You… a pub?" said Lenny in utter disbelief. "You'd drink away the profits." Taffy nodded his head in the agreement. "Yeah… like I said, we all have a dream."

Lenny lay on the sofa dozing. Sue passed him on the way to the kitchen and gave him a smile.

This smile meant Sue was in a good mood and if Sue was in a good mood, maybe now was a good time to ask. Lenny thought to himself.

"Do you fancy going out tonight?"

"Yes, we could do. What's on and WHAT THE FUCKIN' HELL?" Sue came sprinting into the room clutching her chest.

Lenny jumped to his feet. "What… what's the matter?"

Sue pointed to the kitchen. "There's a… there's a… in a bin liner there's a big dead thing."

Lenny became worried. Sue was in danger of losing her good mood, which meant, staying in.

"It's alright, it's alright. I forgot about that. I'll shift it." Lenny searched under the sofa for his shoes. "I'll put it in shed."

"You… you… you've brought a big dead thing into our house?"

"I'm sorry," said Lenny desperately trying to avoid an argument, while fearing one was inevitable.

"What do you want with a big dead thing?"

"It's not a big dead thing," explained Lenny. "It's a lot of little...dead...things."

Lenny couldn't help feeling his explanation was making things worse. Sue looked at him in disbelief, which prompted him to add, "Pigeons!"

"And what are you going to do with them?" asked Sue as her anger gave way to curiosity.

"They're racing pigeons. Bill Murphy gave them to me," Lenny considered for a moment. "Well, sort of, and I'm going to sell them...for money." Lenny expected Sue to look pleased. She didn't. In fact, this seemed to confuse her even more.

"But," she said as if it was Lenny who didn't understand, "they're dead!"

"I know they're dead. I'm not selling them for racing; I'm selling them for their meat," growled Lenny who was now beginning to lose his own temper.

"Meat? Meat? Do you know how many pigeons it takes to make a decent meal?" asked Sue who was now barely able to stop herself from laughing out loud. "Do you?"

"I've got a bloody sack full. How many more do I need?" Lenny snapped back.

Lenny had every reason to be angry; he'd had a bad day. He'd been accused of dishonesty, almost been killed in a car accident, he'd had to pay Robin to retrieve Numbnuts car Key's, and his nose was still hurting. Lenny looked at Sue, saw how happy she was and couldn't help but smile.

It was seven o'clock and in the concert room of the Miner's Welfare, and apart from a couple of old men in the corner, a guy on stage setting up sound equipment and Colin Vine, the place was empty. Colin preferred it this way. He didn't want people asking him awkward questions about why his left leg was in a plaster. He had no idea that word of his suicide attempt was already out. The last thing Colin wanted was for people to find that out. He couldn't bear the thought of people feeling sorry for him, or even worse, people like Titch Ellis finding out and taking the mickey.

Titch Ellis was a very funny man whose loud-mouthed sarcastic humour always made his two cronies (Brian Adams and Bob Fletcher) laugh. To everyone else, however, he was an arse.

Yes, most definitely the last thing Colin wanted was for people like Titch Ellis to find out.

"Oy, Colin," shouted Titch Ellis who had just come in with his two cronies.

Colin looked up, 'Oh My God,' he thought to himself. Titch was standing on his tiptoes with one hand above his head, supposedly to indicate he was holding a piece of rope, his head to one side and his tongue protruding. He was making a loud gurgling noise, and his two cronies were of course, laughing. In fact, the trio laughed out loud all the way to the bar. Colin wished he'd left the club earlier. He had intended going before people started arriving for the cabaret, but he had a lot on his mind and had completely lost track of time.

To Colin's horror, Titch, Brian and Bob made their way to his table and sat down.

"What's this we've been hearing about you trying to top you're sen?" said Titch, obviously faking concern in his voice.

"Piss off Titch."

"Is it true?" asked Bob.

Colin declined to answer.

"Come on Colin," said Brian, "what's happened?"

Again, Colin declined to answer.

"I'll tell you what happened," said Titch as if he knew for a fact. "Colin's mum came home early and caught Colin dressing up in her clothes. Colin here was so embarrassed he went out and tried to hang himself. That's right int it Colin?"

"Fuck off Titch."

"In fact," said Titch, "my source tells me that if you hadn't still been wearing your mum's high heels you would have succeeded."

Brian and Bob laughed themselves senseless as Colin put down his drink and hobbled towards the door.

"Hey, watch where you're going," said Lenny as young Colin barged past him in the foyer.

Sue grabbed her husband's arm. "Leave him. I'll tell you about it later."

Lenny and Sue took their usual table at the back of the room. Gradually, over the next half-hour, the place began to fill up.

Taffy arrived at about ten-to-eight and Numbnuts about thirty seconds later, (both headed straight to the bar).

"Pint of lager please Maureen," said Taffy. Then, noticing another barmaid at the optics shouted, "hey Angie, how do you like your eggs in the morning?"

Angie smiled; it was a long running joke between her and Taffy.

"Unfertilised. Fuck off."

Angie's face dropped as soon as the words left her lips. "Sorry Numbnuts, I didn't see you there."

Numbnuts smiled awkwardly. "That's alright. Could I have a pint of lager please duck? If you're not too busy."

"There's a fuckin' queue you know," said a voice to his left. "Been here ten fuckin' minutes and you come waltzing fuckin in, straight to fuckin front!"

"Now Harry," said Maureen as she took Taffy's money. "What have I told you about swearing at the bar?" Harry grunted an apology.

Taffy and Numbnuts collected their drinks and joined Sue and Lenny at their table at the back of the room.

"Where's Sandra?" asked Sue politely.

"She's still getting ready," replied Numbnuts. "She'll be up in a bit. Have you seen him before?"

Sue took a sip of her Bacardi and coke. "Have I seen who before?"

"Chuck Colorado. He's American."

"Never heard of him, have you Lenny?"

Lenny shook his head. "No, can't say I have."

Lenny's apathy didn't affect Numbnuts' enthusiasm. "Bet he's from New Orleans. That's where all the best Country and Western singers are from."

"I thought that was Blues singers," said Taffy.

Lenny shook his head. "Jazz!"

Taffy and Numbnuts looked confused, and so Lenny reluctantly explained, "New Orleans is the home of Jazz; Nashville is the home of Country and Western."

"I thought Nashville was Jazz."

"No, Country and Western."

Taffy and Numbnuts seemed to accept this for a while until a thought eventually occurred to Taffy. "Where does Blues come from then?"

Lenny, who didn't want to get into this conversation in the first place, decided it was time to get out (he also didn't know the answer). "Shut, up."

"Aye-up," said Taffy from the rim of his pint-pot. "Jabber-jaw's in."

Sue looked up towards the bar and waved; Janet and Jim waved back and made their way over.

"Aye-up luvvy," said Janet with a smile. "Any room?"

Everyone moved round the table to allow Janet and Jim to sit down.

"Your Sandra's on her way up.

"Oh, you've seen her, have you? She said she wouldn't be long."

Janet took a sip from her whiskey glass. "Yes, she's walking up with Georgio."

Numbnuts' look of discomfort went unnoticed by Janet.

"Who's on tonight then?" asked Jim, who had noticed.

"Chuck Colorado," said Lenny, then, pre-empting Jim's next question, added, "Country and Western."

"She's here now look," announced Janet as she began waving. "Told you she was on her way up."

Everyone moved a little further round the table and allowed Sandra to sit down.

"Bloody cold out there," she said as she hung her coat on the back of the chair.

Janet leaned over the table to Sandra. "Have you heard about young Colin?"

Sandra shook her head. "No, what?"

"He tried to top himself today."

“He dint! What made him go and do a thing like that?”

“Who’s tried to top themselves?” interrupted Lenny.

“Colin Vine,” said Sue with an all-knowing nod. “I was going to tell you later.”

“Hear that Taffy?” said Lenny with genuine concern. “Young Colin’s tried to kill himself. Wonder what’s made him do that then.”

“Ooh, I know,” said Sandra with a start. “He’s got an eviction notice served on him last week, bet that’s it.”

Lenny thought for a moment. “I thought he lived with his mam?”

“He does, but Colin took the tenancy over when his dad died.”

“Actually,” announced Janet, “I’ve heard his girlfriend’s left him.”

“Really?” said Taffy. “Is she…er…is she good looking?”

“Too good for thee, Taffy Owen” said Janet sternly.

Lenny wiped some froth from his top lip. “Do many people know about this?”

“Half of the chuffin’ village I should think. You know what it’s like round here for gossip.”

“And where did you get it from?” asked Taffy sarcastically.

Taffy’s sarcasm went straight over Janet’s head. “Gob on a stick… Liz Fisher,” she explained.

Everyone nodded in agreement; they all knew what a gossip Liz was.

“What’s up with you?” asked Sandra as she dug Numbnuts playfully in the ribs.

“Nowt’s up with me.”

“Well, get to bar then.”

Numbnuts stood up and Taffy and Lenny handed their empty pint-pots. Then, noticing Jim’s glass was half-empty, he politely asked, “Shall I get you and Janet one, Jim?”

Jim mulled over his response for a moment before Janet answered for him. “No, we’ll get our own, thanks; we’re not stopping long; we’re going to have an early night.”

Janet squeezed Jim's leg under the table. Jim thought for a moment (this was news to him) then downed his pint and handed the empty glass to Numbnuts.

"Lager please."

Janet folded her arms, sat back in her chair and muttered, "single malt then."

"Aren't we sad?" announced Sue in a very thoughtful way.

The entire table looked at one another. Eventually it was Lenny who had to ask, "what do you mean?"

"Well… look at us. A young lad tries to kill himself and we're almost glad it gives us something to talk about."

"Now hold on a bit," Jim protested. "I wouldn't say anyone was glad young Colin tried to top himself, it's just that… well you know, it's news."

"Yeah, that's what I mean, it's sad."

"It's not sad," said Lenny. "It's bloody depressing. Sue's right. Nothing ever happens round here."

Everyone reflected on this simple but depressing truth.

"What about the armed robbery?" said Jim with a hopeful nod.

"What armed robbery?" asked Lenny.

"The one just outside Manchester, ont' moors… a couple of years ago."

Lenny looked puzzled. "Manchester's forty bloody miles away. How's that come under the category of things that happen around here?"

"Because" interrupted Taffy, who had just realised where Jim was heading with his point, "one of the robbers lived in Brookly, which is only up the road from here."

"Charlie Marshall," said Lenny as he smiled and shook his head. "Do you know, I've been trying all day to remember who I knew from Brookly."

Sue looked a little worried. "Who's Charlie Marshall, and how do you know him?"

"Charlie Marshall was the guy who nicked a million and then turned himself in."

"Not only did he turn himself in, he also turned the whole gang in," added Jim.

"And you know this Charlie character?" asked Sue.

"No, that's just it, I don't know him, I just know of him. That's why I couldn't remember."

"I remember that," said Janet, who had momentarily stopped sulking. "The money's still missing, int' it?"

Jim rubbed his hands together. "A cool million in unmarked notes. I envy the lucky bugger who finds that."

Lenny shook his head. "That money's long gone."

"Where?" asked Jim. "Charlie Marshall turned the whole gang in."

Taffy agreed, "he did."

"So, who's got the money?"

"Mr Big," Lenny said as if it was a well-known fact.

Everyone thought about this for a moment before Sandra asked, "Levi?"

"No, Mr Big, the man at the top, the man who planned the robbery. There's always a Mr Big."

Numbnuts returned to the table with a tray of drinks, just as the lights dimmed and a voice over the loudspeakers said, "*Ladies and gentlemen, put your hands together for, Mr... Chuck... Colorado.*"

The audience clapped enthusiastically as Chuck (complete with a cowboy outfit and an acoustic guitar) walked on stage.

He smiled, raised his hand appreciatively and he spoke into the mic on centre stage. "Ta...ta...thanks fo' that... thank you."

Lenny wondered why he kept thanking everyone; the audience had stopped clapping after Chuck's second ta!

"Av I got sum rait good songs fo' you lot t'neet."

Lenny lowered his head into his hands and wondered how long Barnsley has been the 51st state of America.

Jim looked at Janet, Janet looked at Sue, Sue looked at Sandra, and Numbnuts, in turn, looked at Chuck in disbelief.

Taffy, who was grinning from ear to ear, turned to look at everyone and said, "Now that's what I call a cowboy!"

"Am gonner start wi this'un. It's from a bloke called Kenny Rodgers, an it's called, 'You picked a fine time to leave mi Looseal', an it guz summat like this..."

After the second verse of 'You picked a fine time to leave mi Looseal' Numbnuts noticed that Chuck's singing voice wasn't all that bad and decided to share his observation with Lenny.

"Actually, he wouldn't be a bad singer... if he kept his gob shut."

I beg you to reconsider wrote Charlie Marshall. *I know we have been apart for some time, and I realise we never parted on the best terms, but I beg you not to do this thing. I am up for parole next year and if you would only give me one more chance, I promise you things will be alright. I cannot say too much as all my letters are vetted, but I swear things will be different for us if you would only wait a little longer before making your decision. You don't know what this will do to me, you are the only one...* Charlie broke off from writing and turned his letter face down as his cellmate entered the cell.

"I've got a date," said Peter Bellis holding up a letter of his own. "The week before Christmas."

Charlie tried to force a smile. "That's great. You got anywhere to stop?"

"I've got a sister in Manchester who says I can spend a little time with her, you know, until I get on my own two feet."

"That's great." Charlie folded up his own letter and put it in his pocket before laying on his bed.

Peter re-read his release papers several times and was only interrupted by a prison guard who checked on the room before locking the cell door. A short time after that, a bell rang, and a short time after that, the cell lights were turned out.Peter lay in the darkness thinking of Christmas at home and was unable to see the look of worry on his cellmate's face.

Chapter Three

You May As Well Be Hung For a Sheep

Colin quietly opened the door to his living room. His mother turned away from the TV and smiled. This took a great deal of effort for Mrs Vine; she wasn't a well woman.

Vera Vine had had her one and only son, Colin, late in life. She had always been a relatively fit and healthy woman until four years ago, when her husband (Colin's father) passed away. Vera Vine had taken her husband's death very badly and was now addicted to several kinds of medication, originally designed to help her through her bereavement. It was this cocktail of drugs, as much as her own broken heart that was now slowly but surely killing her.

"Hello love. Ooh, what have you been doing?" Vera was looking at Colin's plaster pot.

"I told you this afternoon Mam, I hurt it playing football."

"Oh, I don't know. Always in the wars, aren't you? Never mind, your father will be in soon. He'll know best what to do with it. "

Memory loss was one of the side effects of Vera's medication, and a condition that Colin sometimes wished upon himself.

"I'm going to have a nice cup of cocoa before bed. Shall I make you one?"

"No thanks Mum, I'm going to take a bath."

"Alright love, see you in the morning." Vera turned to the TV screen.

"Mum," said Colin, entering the room for the first time.

"What love?" answered Vera with a smile as Colin perched himself on the arm of the chair.

Colin paused for a moment; there was so much he wanted to tell her, so much he wanted her to understand. He looked into his mother's face for a moment and could see that contentment in her ignorance.

"Nothing. Goodnight Mum." Colin bent over and kissed his mother's cheek.

"You're not going to bed, are you? I was just going to make a cup of cocoa."

Colin gave his mother's hand a gentle squeeze. "Good night, Mum."

Vera smiled at Colin as he left the room, then turned back to the TV and forgot about the cocoa. Colin closed the bathroom door and turned on the taps. He removed his clothes then leant over the bathroom sink. As he looked up, he saw his own face staring back at him in the mirrored cabinet on the wall. He watched as condensation formed on the glass until there was no longer a Colin Vine staring back at him. He opened the cabinet door, took out a bottle of his mother's pills and poured himself a glass of water. Then he climbed into the bath. Resting his pot between the bath taps, he wolfed down half a dozen pills, then he laid back and closed his eyes. He thought about his mother, a subject he'd thought about a lot lately. He had it all planned. With no more Colin Vine, the authorities would have to take his mother into care. The insurance would pay up and that would ensure that she wanted for nothing, except maybe a son... No, that wouldn't happen (Colin preferred to think). She had forgotten about his father's death; she would forget about his.

Colin felt a sudden pain across his abdomen; it disappeared as quickly as it had appeared. His girlfriend, Julie, had certainly got her wish: she had told Colin she never wanted to see him again.

Lying perfectly still, he closed his eyes. The bath water came to rest without a ripple and he felt warm, comfortable and at ease.

Suddenly Colin was startled by a knock on the door.

"Colin, are you in there?"

"Yes mum. I'm just having... ooh (there was that pain again) ... a bath."

"Only I can't find my laxatives. I think they're in the bathroom cabinet. Could you just have a look for me?"

Lenny stood at the kitchen sink. He had spent all morning plucking and gutting pigeons, but now, as he held in the palm of his hand the last of the thirty-two birds, he had to admit to himself that Sue had been right: it was going to take a lot of these to make a decent meal.

The birds that were lined up along the draining board reminded him of plums. They were about the right size and shape, over-ripened maybe, but plums nevertheless. Lenny felt a little disappointed. He wasn't going to be able to sell these for as much as he had hoped. Still, he thought, looking at the last pigeon, a bird in the hand, so to speak, must be worth a couple of bob.

"What's that?" said Lisa as she tugged his trouser leg.

Lenny had been so engrossed in his morning's work that he hadn't noticed Lisa's entrance. An easy thing to do you would think, given that Lisa was a shy and well-behaved five-year-old and as her godfather, (Numbnuts) often said, was as quiet as a butcher's dog (but then again Numbnuts often got his similes mixed up). Lenny almost never missed anything Lisa did. She was the apple of his eye.

"That," said Lenny, as he placed the bird on a saucer and presented it to his daughter, "it's a Christmas turkey for Santa's elves."

Lisa studied it for a moment before asking, "will there be enough?"

"Of course there will be enough," Lenny crouched down and held his hand about a foot off the ground. "Don't forget, Santa's elves are only this big."

Lisa stopped wiping the sleep from her eyes and became a little excited, "Santa's coming to my school soon."

Lenny scooped his daughter up with one hand and gave her a hug. "That's right, and I expect he'll be bringing presents for all the children who have been good."

Lisa nodded in agreement and put her arms around her father's neck.

Lenny's smile faded a little as he noticed Sue leaning against the kitchen door.

There was a certain look about her; she was smiling but at the same time a little distant as if deep in thought.

"You alright?" asked Lenny.

"Actually," said Sue, "there's been a bit of a hiccup with this year's party."

"What kind of hiccup?"

Sue walked over and playfully pinched her daughter's cheek. "Have you opened your advent calendar this morning?" she asked.

Lisa shook her head,

"Well, you'd better go and do it."

Lenny put Lisa down and watched as she ran excitedly into the living room.

"What hiccup?" Lenny repeated.

"Well, you know Mr Grayson who usually does the Santa."

"Yeah."

"Well, his kidneys have packed in. You know how much he used to drink... Anyway, that's another story. Point is the school hasn't got a Santa this year."

"Can't they get someone else to do it?" asked Lenny anxiously.

Who? People don't seem to have the time; you know how it is."

Lenny became a little annoyed. "Don't have the time! Half the bleeding village is on strike. Course people have got the time."

"Can't be bothered then."

Lenny took out a handful of carrier bags from the kitchen cupboard. "Can't be bothered, that's more like it. You'd think one of the parents would do it, wunt yer?"

Sue watched Lenny place the last of the pigeons into the last of the carrier bags and rinse his hands.

"I mean," said Lenny, "it's Christmas. You can't let kids down at Christmas."

Sue smiled. She knew she had him. "Still, you know what men are like."

"No," said Lenny, throwing her hand towel on the draining board as if it were a gauntlet. "I don't know what men are like. I'm a man and there isn't anything I wouldn't do for my kid."

Lenny turned to face his accuser and found her holding a large red... something in front of her face. Sue's fingertips loosened their grip and the large red something unrolled itself and Lenny stood silently staring at a beautiful crimson red Santa's outfit, complete with a belt and a fur trim. Sue lowered the garment from her face and Lenny shook his head and smiled. She was wearing a long white beard.

Lenny struggled to open the doors leading to the bar of the Miner's Institute It wasn't easy; he had put down two of the carrier bags full of dead pigeons and wedge the door open with his foot. Eventually, he made it through and walked confidently up to the bar area, the busiest part of the pub.

"Have I got a bargain for you lot," he announced to a group of about eight men who were gathered around idly talking.

Just as Lenny spoke three men sitting at a nearby table caught his attention. Bill Murphy was shaking his head as Taffy seemed to be explaining something to him; Numbnuts was beckoning Lenny to join them. Lenny had a gut feeling and didn't like it very much.

"I'll be back in a minute boys," said Lenny as he nervously left the group.

Lenny joined his three friends and asked in almost a whisper, "What's wrong?"

"There's been some sort of mistake, hic."

Taffy's hiccups indicated to Lenny that he had been drinking all morning.

Bill coughed loudly, and then managed to catch his breath again. "No mistake. I tell you I've been up and fed them this morning."

"Fed what? What's he talking about?"

Taffy shook his head. "He reckons he's been up to feed his pigeons this morning."

"And?"

"And he reckons they're still there. Hic."

Lenny looked at Numbnuts, then at Taffy, then back to Bill. "They can't have been, we took them yesterday."

"Don't know what you took yesterday. All my birds were sat on their loft this morning waiting to be fed. I fed them myself; our David was busy."

"But... but," stuttered Lenny. "We went... we went up yesterday to the allotment... to your loft... the big blue one at the far end."

Bill looked confused. "Blue one you say... at the far end. That's not my loft."

Lenny and Taffy looked straight at Numbnuts.

"But I saw him there." Numbnuts grabbed Bill's arm as if to plead with him. "I saw you there. I saw you one morning... I walked to work one morning, and you were coming out; you were coming out that loft."

Bill thought for a moment before coming up with a feasible explanation. "I was probably borrowing some corn or something. Maybe I need some advice. I don't know. I suppose I could have just been visiting." Bill's final words deteriorated into a long hard cough.

Lenny sat with his head in his hands trying to think things through.

It was Taffy who eventually had to ask. "Visiting who? Whose loft is it then?"

Bill removed his handkerchief from his mouth and pointed to a large, bearded man who had just entered the club. "His."

Lenny, Taffy and Numbnuts were horrified to see a large, bearded, red-faced mountain of the man making his way to their table.

Haystacks Mckenzy, although a loner, was well known throughout the village mainly because of his striking resemblance to a very famous professional wrestler of the day (hence his name). He kept himself to himself, hunted a lot, and bred greyhounds and pigeons. Apart from that, nothing more was really known about Haystacks. It was rumoured that he was the natural father of Levi, though this was probably not true, as that particular rumour had been traced back to Liz Fisher!

Haystacks leant his gun case against the wall and pulled up a chair. "Here Bill, you an't seen any strangers round allotments lately, have you?"

"No. Why? What's wrong?"

"Some bastards had away with my birds, that's what."

Bill looked at Lenny. "Oh dear."

"They've took the fuckin' lot they have. Bastards!"

"Bastards," agreed Lenny, pushing one of the carrier bags under the table with his foot. There was an awkward moment of silence as the guilty parties wondered what they could say that would proclaim their innocence; phrases like 'well it wasn't us' were out of the question.

"Well, it wasn't us," said Numbnuts.

Haystacks looked at Numbnuts as if he had just said something profoundly stupid.

"I know it wasn't you. What do you know about pigeons? No, these were professionals."

"Professional what?" asked Lenny.

"Professional criminals."

Lenny couldn't understand Haystacks' reasoning, but he was glad he was on the wrong track. Still, he had to ask, "why would professional criminals want to steal your pigeons Haystacks?"

"That's what I mean; you lot know nowt about pigeons. Some of them birds were worth thousands. I've got two... I had two, all England winners in that lot, and a one-year-old cock that would have probably made champion next year. Bastards."

"Have you told the Police?" asked Bill nervously.

"He dunt want to involve Police," Lenny interjected almost immediately.

Haystacks looked up at Taffy and Numbnuts who were shaking their heads most definitely and uttering things like, "No, not the Police," and "I wouldn't, hic, involve them, no."

"No," said Haystacks, reaching over to his gun case and pulling it to his side. "I'll sort it out myself." Haystacks gave his gun a little pat.

"I'd call the Police," said Lenny.

Taffy and Numbnuts nodded in agreement. "Yeah, let them deal with it. Police, yes, definite, hic."

Suddenly Taffy had an idea. "What if they ant been nicked?"

"What do you mean?" Haystacks hadn't considered any other possibilities.

"It could have been a fox, hic."

Lenny liked this. "Yes, a fox. I've heard that if a fox gets in, it dunt just kill one bird, it goes for lot!"

"That's true," said Haystacks, then paused for a moment to consider the possibility. "No, no, the door was latched shut, a fox couldn't have got in."

"Are you sure?" said Lenny as he eagerly tried to sell the theory. "It could have opened the latch with its paw or something. Clever little fuckers foxes you know."

Haystacks ran his fingers through his beard. "Well, this fucker must have been; it made itself a cup of tea, finished my crossword and latched the door shut again on its way out!"

"Oy, Lenny!" called a voice from behind. Lenny turned and froze. Three of the men had left the bar and were making their way over.

"What have you got for us then?" asked one of them.

"Let's have a look," said another.

"Err, yes, well, that's right" said Lenny as he picked up the carrier bags. "We... er, we were just about to go and get them... err it, weren't we lads?"

Taffy and Numbnuts stood up and put on their coats rather hurriedly. "Yes we... we'll go and get them, shall we?"

A few minutes later, Lenny, Taffy and Numbnuts were walking at a brisk pace down Oakwood Road towards the church.

"What are we going to do now? Hic."

"Shut up. I'm thinking," snapped Lenny as he hopped over the church wall and into the graveyard.

"We'll have to give em back," said Numbnuts as he negotiated the wall in a rather less elegant fashion.

Lenny stopped in his tracks. "Give em back! Give em fucking back!" Lenny began taking pigeons from the carrier bags and throwing them at Numbnuts, "Here, you give em fuckin' back!"

About after the third or fourth pigeon, Taffy was able to calm Lenny down a little and the onslaught of dead pigeons stopped.

Lenny walked a little way into the churchyard and sat on one of the benches that lined the edge of the path. Taffy gave Numbnuts a reassuring pat on the back and they both nervously joined him.

"I don't know," said Lenny as he stared out amongst the crosses, tombstones and angels marking the graves that lay scattered around within the churchyard walls. "Every time we get a break, something spoils it. It's as if someone up there's got something against us." Lenny reflected for a while before continuing. "Do you know what our Susan was doing when I married her?"

"She was training to be a teacher," said Numbnuts solemnly.

"Yeah, loves kids. But she decided to take five years out so we could have one of our own, so that's what she did. Seemed like a good idea at the time. I was earning enough money; there would have been no problem paying for the rest of her education. So, last year, she applied for a place at teacher training college, got accepted too." Lenny hung his head. "Didn't tell me she was accepted. I came across it when I was sorting out some bills we couldn't pay. It was dated the 6th of March."

"The same day the strike started," said Taffy.

"The same fuckin' day! So, she turned the placement down and never said a word about it. She still dunt know that I know."

Numbnuts sympathised. "You'll get there, maybe next year, aye, when strike's over."

Lenny got up and walked over to one of the graves. The inscription on the marble headstone simply read *Elizabeth Anne Marshall. Born 1932. Died 1981. My Queen.* Lenny didn't know Elizabeth Anne Marshall, but her headstone seemed to sum up everything for Lenny. He knew all his hopes and dreams would come to nothing. He knew one day he would lie somewhere out here with nothing to say for himself, nothing to show, nothing to be remembered for. Elizabeth Anne Marshall, she was born and then she died.

"A loved one, is it?"

Lenny turned and saw the familiar figure of Father Patrick O'Connor walking down the path leading to the church.

"No Father," Lenny turned and looked at the inscription one last time. "It's nobody."

"You boys are not looking for me, are you? Only I was just on my way to see Mrs Daniels. Her husbands really poorly you know.

Lenny shook his head. "No Father, we were just passing through."

Father O'Connor paused briefly and looked at the grave, and then he nodded his head. "Aren't we all, my son, aren't we all?"

Father O'Connor made the sign of a cross on his chest and left via the main gate at the front of the church.

"Come on," said Taffy. "Let's get out of here."

Taffy, Numbnuts and Lenny continued through the churchyard and exited through the back gate. They crossed the old footbridge to and headed up towards the lake.

The boards of the jetty creaked under Lenny's weight as he walked out to its end.

"What are you doing?" asked Numbnuts from the safety of the embankment.

Lenny didn't answer immediately; instead, he threw the carrier bags into the semi frozen waters of the boating lake. The splash startled a couple of ducks into flight, and they quacked their way off into the distance. Water found its way into the bags; after a few seconds they were gone. Lenny turned and walked back along the jetty with his hands in his pockets.

"It's called getting rid of the evidence."

Lenny joined Numbnuts who was sitting on the embankment wall. Taffy remained standing, preferring to kick the concrete rubbish bin in an attempt to get some feeling back into his toes.

"Stupid fuckin' idea," uttered Lenny as he pulled out his tobacco tin. Taffy stopped kicking the bin and stood silent for a moment.

"Actually, it wasn't, was it?"

"What are you talking about?" asked Numbnuts. "At best the Police are going to be after us, at worse we're going to be shot."

"I know," said Taffy who now for some unknown reason had suddenly become positively excited, "but the idea of selling fresh meat that you get for free, at a cheap price to people who can't afford shop prices, is good."

Lenny noted that Taffy's hiccups had thankfully subsided. "If you're thinking about Bill's pigeons, forget it. We touch them, Haystacks is sure to suss out what happened."

"No. Fuck the pigeons, scrawny little bastard things. Think big. We're only ten miles from the moors." Taffy's face was beaming, even when a look of horror came across Lenny's.

"No way. No fucking way."

"What's he talking about?" asked Numbnuts.

"He's talking about sheep rustling, that's what he's talking about."

"Think about it," said Taffy as wide-eyed as ever. "Leg of lamb, lamb shanks, lamb chops. We could make thirty or forty quid a time."

"Hang on," said Numbnuts as if he was about to throw a fly into Taffy's ointment. "Aren't lambs born in the spring?"

Taffy remained undeterred. "That doesn't matter. We just pick one out that's come from this year's young; it's only going to be six or seven months old at best. The meat's still tender at that age. Trust me I know about sheep, I'm Welsh!"

"I'm in," said Numbnuts.

"Good. When shall we go?"

"No time like the present."

"What, now?"

"No, tonight. I'm busy this afternoon."

"Just a minute you two," said Lenny in an effort to calm both Taffy and Numbnuts down a little. "Think what you're getting yourselves in to. It's a criminal offence, you know. What if you get caught?"

Taffy almost laughed. "What, a couple of starving miners bag a sheep to feed their starving families at Christmas. They're hardly going to lock us up and throw away the key, are they? Press would have a field day. Anyway, we won't get caught; there won't be anyone up there to catch us. What fuckin' idiot would go wandering around up there, in the dead of night, this time of year?"

"He's right, you'd have to be mad," said Numbnuts. "Are you in?"

"I can't. Our Sue would kill me if she found out."

"You really think a lot about her, don't you? Said Taffy quietly.

"You know I do."

"So, what have you got her for Christmas then?"

"Nothing yet. You know damn well I haven't got any mon…" Lenny stopped talking as he realised what Taffy's point was.

"Look, think about it. We'll be leaving Numbnuts' place at what? Eight o'clock?"

Numbnuts nodded in agreement.

Lenny shook his head. "I'll think about it."

Janet pushed her trolley past the cake and biscuit section of Tesco's supermarket. She was on a budget and there was nothing down that aisle that was on her list. 'Anyway', she told herself, 'I'm on a diet; just a piece of meat and some veg', she reminded herself. "What can I get you?" asked a tall, skinny, acne-faced lad at the meat counter. Janet looked at the name badge, which was pinned to his apron.

"I don't know… er Gary; I don't know what I fancy."

"Some meat I hope."

"Too bloody right," Janet had spoken out without thinking and was now a little embarrassed. "I mean, that's right, I want some meat but I'm not sure what meat I want, just something for my old man's tea really."

"How about a couple of lamb chops?"

"Lamb chops! Some of us are on strike you know. Give us a pound of brisket."

Gary took out a large piece of meat and started cutting.

"Hello Janet," said Liz Fisher who happened to be passing the meat counter.

"Hello Liz," Janet smiled politely. "What's new?"

Liz pulled her trolley to a halt. "I told you about young Colin, didn't I?"

Janet nodded expectantly.

"Well, that's about it really." Liz thought for a moment. "Ooh except, did you know Levi's got a new job?"

"No, I saw him yesterday, he didn't say anything." Janet paused to recollect. "He had a nice suit on though. What's he doing?"

"Don't know. He's been very secretive about the whole thing. Makes you wonder though, dunt it?"

Janet nodded and wondered. "Yeah, strange, isn't it? Seems to me everyone's laying off around here; strike seems to be affecting everybody."

"Well, better get off," said Liz with a smile.

"Yes, see you later luvvy."

"There you are, Madam, that's just over. Is that alright for you?"

Janet looked at the price of the meat that was being presented to her. "Yes, that'll do."

Gary put the meat in a bag, sealed it and placed a sticker on it. "There you go, that'll put lead in his pencil."

Gary's friendly smile diminished somewhat in the wake of Janet's reaction to his off-the-cuff comment.

"What do you mean it will put lead in his pencil? He's got enough lead in his pencil, thank you very much. There's nothing wrong with his pencil."

Gary looked a little confused. "No, I just meant... well, it's just a saying. You know, it's full of proteins and vitamins and stuff. It's good for you, gives you energy, you know? It'll put lead in his pencil!"

Janet reluctantly accepted his explanation and Gary handed her the pound of brisket.

"On second thoughts," said Janet as she turned to make sure Liz Fisher hadn't been in ear shot of the conversation, "better make it two poun".

Chapter Four

Murder On The Moors

Lenny placed his hand on the piece of paper that Lisa had provided, and Lisa outlined it.

"That's very good. Now shall we do yours?"

"No, we haven't done your nails."

Lenny smiled. "Ok then. You draw the nails and then I'll do your hand."

Lisa exchanged the pink marker pen she had used to outline her father's hand for a bright red one.

"Red! I haven't got red fingernails."

Lisa put pen to paper. "You're wearing nail vanish."

Lenny laughed. "Do you mean nail varnish, like what mummy wears?"

Lisa nodded and carried on with her picture.

"Don't get ink on that table you two," shouted a voice from the kitchen.

"We're not babies you know," answered Lenny, smiling down at his daughter.

Lisa smiled back as she placed the tip of her handkerchief in her mouth, and then used it to rub out the smudged her father had made on the walnut veneer.

"Daddy, draw me a bike," said Lisa, pushing a clean sheet of paper to her father.

"What kind of bike?"

"A pink one."

"A pink one? Pink is for girls," said Lenny mockingly.

Lisa laughed, "I am a girl."

"Are you? I thought you were a boy."

Lisa laughed again. "No, silly, I'm a girl."

"Ok then, a pink one."

Lenny began to draw a pink bike.

"With a bell on it."

Lenny added a bell.

"And a basket."

Lenny added a basket.

"There we are, a pink bike with a bell and a basket."

Lisa looked at the picture in silence; she had also stopped smiling.

"Is there something wrong?" asked Lenny.

Lisa shook her head.

"Don't you like it?"

Lisa nodded.

"What's wrong then?"

"She wants a bike for Christmas," said Sue, who was leaning against the kitchen door with her arms full of washing. "I've told her we can't afford it." Sue hung her head and then disappeared back into the kitchen.

Lisa was still staring at the picture.

"Well," said Lenny as cheerfully as he could, and then found he had nothing to say. Eventually the phrase, "Maybe next year," found his way to his lips.

Lisa nodded then left the table and went to her room.

Lenny picked up the picture of the pink bike and looked at it for a short while before screwing it up and putting his head in his hands.

Sue had just turned the washing machines dial to D when she heard the click of the front door. She put down the washing powder and went to investigate.

The front room was empty, but through the bay window she could see her husband pulling on his coat as he walked off up the garden path.

Sue picked up the screwed picture of the pink bike and unfolded it, she wondered about her husband, and worried.

"Ok then," said Taffy as he emerged from Numbnuts' front door, "maybe George Best didn't play in a World Cup, but if he did, he would have blinded Bobby fucking Charlton."

Numbnuts nudged Taffy and pointed up the garden path towards Lenny who was sitting on Sally's bonnet smoking a cigarette.

"Told you he wouldn't let us down," whispered Taffy as he opened the garden gate.

"You're coming then?" asked Numbnuts in an uncertain tone.

"Aye, why not?"

"See," said Taffy. "Told you he'd come. What did I tell you?"

Lenny looked nervous or at least a little uncertain or that's how it appeared to Numbnuts.

"Look, are you sure about this?"

"Course he's sure, aren't you Lenny?"

Lenny put out his cigarette. "Yes, I'm sure. Come on, let's go."

Numbnuts opened the car doors, and everyone climbed in.

"So," said Taffy as Sally pulled away. "Who do you think was the world's best striker? George Best or Bobby Charlton?"

Lenny wasn't really listening; he had just noticed something very curious through one of Sally's wing mirrors and was asking himself what Georgio was doing hanging around the corner at this time of night.

"Well?" pressed Taffy.

"Well, what?"

"Who was the best striker, George Best or Bobby Charlton?"

Lenny considered for a moment. "Pele."

"Fuckin' Pele! George Best, any day."

Sally passed the last streetlight and disappeared into the night.

"I'm telling you it was Pele."

"Bobby Charlton."

"Pele."

"George Best."

"What about Bobby Moore?"

Jim Mulligan was sitting rolling cigarettes at the kitchen as he patiently waited for his tea.

"Don't roll them there," Janet commanded as she entered the dining room, carrying two cooked dinners. "You'll get 'bacca' everywhere."

"So?"

"So, you'll get it in your dinner, and I've made summat special."

Janet set the two dinners down and smiled proudly. Jim put away his tobacco tin and suspiciously prodded his dinner with his fork.

"What is it?"

"Brisket."

"What's brisket?"

"It's sort of cheap beef."

Jim took his first mouthful. "Hmm, all right is this."

Janet's proud smile returned.

"A bit tough mind you." Jim noticed his wife's smile begin to weaken and quickly added, "nice though."

Janet smiled with more intensity than ever. "And there's four cans of John smiths int' fridge for later."

"Bloody hell. What have I done to deserve this?"

"Nothing yet," Janet winked at Jim and Jim found it hard to swallow his brisket.

When the meal was over, Janet cleared the table and asked, "Do you want a beer?"

"Yeah, go on then."

She took away the pots. She returned a few minutes later and handed Jim a cold can of John Smiths bitter before settling beside him on the settee.

"Are you tired?" enquired Jim.

Janet rested her head on his lap and smiled up at him. "No."

"Do you feel ill?"

"No."

"Then why have you put your nighty on?"

"I thought I might have an early night."

"You said you weren't tired." Jim looked at his watch. "It's only twenty-past eight."

Janet sat up sharply and folded her arms. "You don't have to be tired to use the chuffin bed you know." Janet expected some sort of response from her husband, she wasn't quite sure what, but she definitely expected something. An apology would be nice. None came. Janet started at Jim and began to wonder if it was her own sex appeal that was at fault or whether she had married a man who was too thick to take a hint. She hoped for the latter and decided to give it another go. "I was hoping you were going to join me." Janet again awaited response from. Jim sat on the edge of his seat with an excited look in his eyes, which gave her a great deal of encouragement. Janet sat forward too.

"Go on my son," cried Jim.

Janet got up and turned off the TV.

"What are you doing? We were about to score," protested Jim.

"Have you been listening to a word I've been saying?"

Jim seemed perplexed at Janet's fury. "Yes, you want an early night. That's alright love." Jim rose to his feet. "I've got to go down to Kenny's anyway. He wants me to see to his engine.

Jim kissed Janet on the forehead. "Go on, you get to bed. I'll see you in the morning."

As Jim opened his garden gate, he thought, just for a moment, that he'd heard a scream. Or was it the wind? Jim closed the gate and set off down the road to Kenny's.

The conversation had gone from football to politics to the miners' strike back to football on to Miss World (via George Best) and was currently on current affairs.

"So," said Numbnuts, "these IRA blokes, how do they expect to get off with it by refusing to recognise the courts?"

"They didn't," explained Lenny. "They were trying to make a political statement."

"Right," said Numbnuts. "Which was, what?"

"Well, they didn't refuse to recognise the courts; they said they failed to recognise this court, meaning the Old Bailey."

"Why?"

"Well, the Old Bailey is a British Court, and they don't consider themselves to be British."

"Well," said Numbnuts slowly, "what do they consider themselves to be?"

"Irish," interjected Taffy.

"They *are* Irish."

"But they're from Northern Ireland," explained Lenny, "which makes them British, and they don't want to be British."

"The bombings were carried out on the British mainland; it wouldn't have mattered if they were classed as Outer Mongolians, they would still be tried here."

Numbnuts shook his head. "I don't get it."

"It's like I said, they were trying to make a statement! You want to be left at the roundabout? There's a pub about two hundred yards up."

Taffy smiled, "A pub?"

"We're not having a drink, you Prick. It's got a car park round the back with a public footpath out onto the moors. Me and Sue used to come up here in summer, you know, for picnics and that."

"I know what a picnic is. It's the 'and that' I'd like to know more about."

"Fuck off Taffy. There, park against that wall."

Sally purred to a halt. The three men got out and quietly closed the doors. Lenny surveyed the area the best he could; it was very dark. The lights were on in the pub, but the curtains were drawn. There were two more cars and a lorry in the car park but they were empty. "Perfect," said Lenny to himself.

Taffy and Numbnuts were halfway over the stile leading to the open moor when Lenny whispered after them, "Oy, aren't you forgetting something?" They looked at each other and shrugged.

"The gun."

Numbnuts and Taffy climbed back over the stile. "What gun?" asked Numbnuts.

"The gun to shoot the sheep."

"I never thought about that."

"Fuckin brilliant!" exclaimed Lenny. "I'm working with two criminal masterminds."

"Well, I don't own a gun. Do you, Taff?"

"No, never have."

Lenny sat on the stile to think. Taffy began kicking one of the stile posts and Numbnuts leaned back on Sally and began to rub his chin.

"You're Welsh," said Numbnuts eventually. "You should know how to kill a sheep. How do you do it in Wales?"

"We shoot them."

After a minute or two of contemplation, Taffy stopped kicking the post. "We could just hit it over the head with something."

"I've got a tyre spanner in the car."

"Not heavy enough," said Taffy who had suddenly become an expert on killing sheep. "Quite a touchy little creature is a sheep. We need something heavier, something like a decent piece of four-by-four." Taffy stopped talking and turned to look at the post he had been kicking and smiled.

After twenty-five minutes of pulling and pushing at the post, the three men were exhausted, and the post remained intact. They decided to sit on the stile to rethink their strategy.

"That's it," said Lenny. "Let's get off home.

"We can't give up now; we're too close," protested Numbnuts.

"Too close? Too close?" Lenny began to raise his voice and was reminded of the fact by Taffy. "We've been here half-a-fuckin'-hour, and we haven't left the fuckin' car park, and if we did, we probably wouldn't catch a sheep. They don't just stand around and let people belt them with a piece of -four-by-four you know.

"They do," said Taffy who then thought he had better explain. "Well, maybe not let you belt them over the head, but they do stand still if you shine a light on them. It blinds them you see; can't see where they're going so they freeze. So, all we need is that post. Now you two stand to one side."

Taffy took a few paces backwards and took up the pose of an Olympic high jumper, body swaying to and fro, eyes fixed firmly on the post.

"What's he doing?" whispered Numbnuts. Lenny shrugged his shoulders.

"It's okay boys, I've seen them do this on Sunday afternoon wrestling." With that, he took his run up and launched a flying drop kick at the post.

Lenny and Numbnuts stared down at Taffy who was rolling around in agony on the floor.

"Right," said Lenny, "I'm off." Lenny started off towards the car.

Numbnuts called after him, "We can't give up now. I've got a spade in the boot; we'll dig the post out."

Lenny stopped dead in his tracks. "You've got a spade in the boot?"

Numbnuts sensed by Lenny's tone that there was some significance to his admitting to having a spade in the boot, but he didn't know what. "Well, yes… I put one in. In case we got trapped in snow… or something."

"You've got a spade in the boot?"

Lenny trudged on about as fast as you can over moorland in the dead of night (but there again he had the torch). Numbnuts tried to keep up. Taffy, who was at the rear with a smaller torch of his own, stopped occasionally to take a practice swing with the spade. It didn't worry Taffy that Lenny was getting further and further in front. He knew Lenny would stop and ask his opinion when he spotted another sheep. Something Lenny had done twice already. The pub lights were just visible in the distance when Lenny stopped for a third time.

"What about that one?"

Lenny's torch beam had fallen on a sheep beside on of the dry-stone walls that covered the countryside.

Taffy hurried forwards to get a better look. "That's a young un'. That'll do," whispered Taffy.

"What do we do now?"

"You keep the torch on him. Me and Numbnuts will come in from either side. Here, hold this."

Taffy handed Lenny the torch, then he and Numbnuts slipped away into the night. After a few minutes, Lenny spotted Numbnuts a couple of metres to the sheep's right, then Taffy to his left. Lenny kept the torch fixed on the sheep. He could feel his heart beating in his chest as he watched his friends work their way closer and closer to their prey. Suddenly, the sheep's eyes, which had been staring back at him, broke away as it looked to it's right. The animal had obviously heard something moving in the grass, but it was too late. Taffy took the opportunity to strike whilst it's head was turned. In a matter of seconds, he had wrestled it to the ground. Lenny ran over as quickly as he possibly could, stumbling once or twice over the uneven ground.

"You did it! You did it!" he panted out on his arrival. Taffy sat on the floor with the sheep in his lap, his left hand across it's chest and his right hand gripping it's snout.

"Put the light back on it, it'll calm down" he commanded.

Lenny switched the light back on and the sheep stopped struggling.

"Right, what now Taffy?"

"Hit it."

Lenny thought for a moment then handed the spade to Numbnuts. "Hit it, Danny."

Numbnuts seemed a little taken aback. He wasn't at all sure that he could. "Me?" he blurted, "Why me?"

"Because he's holding the sheep and I'm holding the torch."

Numbnuts reluctantly took the spade and brought it up above his head before lowering it down again. "I can't; it's looking at me."

"Of course it's looking at you," growled Taffy. "You're about to smash its fuckin' brains in. Just hit it."

Numbnuts once more raised the spade, held it above his head then lowered it again.

"Can't you cover its eyes up?"

Taffy gritted his teeth in anger but managed to slide his hand up the animal's snout and over it's eyes. "Now, FUCKIN' HIT IT!"

Numbnuts lifted the spade for the last time. Then, closing his eyes, he brought it down hard. There was a dull metallic thud as the spade made contact. Numbnuts opened his eyes slowly to observe the damage he had inflicted, then in a solemn and apologetic voice he spoke. "Sorry Taff."

Taffy was rolling around on the floor with blood on his shirt (his own blood). He had tucked his broken hand under his armpit and was kicking his feet in pain and frustration.

Lenny had acted quickly and had grabbed the sheep by one of its back legs as it tried to make its escape. He was stretched out on the ground with the frightened animal struggling for its life, but his grip remained firm. "DANNY," he shouted, "HIT IT!"

Numbnuts ran over and brought the spade down for a second attempt. This time his aim was good, and the sheep lay motionless on the ground.

Chapter Five

The Fart Squad

Henry West retired from the Navy in 1970 and had used his Navy pension to purchase the tenancy of 'The Lonely Shepherd'. His wife, Mary, happened to be a very good cook and together Henry and Mary had built up a successful business serving reasonably priced bar meals to lorry drivers and such like passing between Sheffield and Manchester on the A57. Henry had waved off his last customer, an overweight Scottish trucker by the name of Allan at about 10:30 that night. That was when he had first noticed a Ford Mustang parked in the far corner of the car park. This had intrigued Henry who over the course of the last hour had been periodically looking through the cracks in the curtains impatiently awaiting the owner's return.

"Come away," said Mary as she emptied the ashtrays into a bucket, "and stop being nosey."

"But whose is it?"

"Probably broken down or something."

Henry thought for a while. "If it's broken down, where is the driver? Are you sure no one has come in to use the phone or anything?"

"No, I've told you, the only people I've seen tonight were those two couples and the Scots man."

Henry left the window and helped his wife set the tables. "Something dodgy there."

"What do you mean dodgy?"

"Well, who would drive up here at this time of night and then just abandon their car?"

"I don't know. Look if it's still there in the morning you can ring the Police. Now make sure you switch the lights off." Mary lifted the access flap to the bar and took off her apron. "Are you coming to bed or what?"

Henry was back at the window. "Yes, I sup…" Henry broke short his sentence.

"Hello…"

"What is it?"

"Someone's here. Quick, turn the lights out."

Mary reluctantly did as her husband had bid. "Who is it?"

"Three blokes. They've just come in from the field. They're going over to the car. They're carrying something. It looks like..." Henry's face went white. He turned to his wife and lowered his voice. "A body!"

Mary hurried over to another window and carefully pulled back the curtain. Through the small gap she had created, Mary could clearly see three men gathered round the boot of the Ford Mustang. Three men appeared to be having some sort of argument and lying at their feet... "Oh my God!" her husband was right... a body!

One of the men opened up the boot and threw in his spade before helping one of the other men pick up the dead body by its arms and legs. The body was manhandled into the boot and the boot was shut.

"What are we going to do?" asked Mary.

There was no answer from her husband; he was busy dialling a number on the cordless phone he had retrieved from behind the bar.

"Hello... which service?" "Err... Police."

There was a pause before Henry spoke again.

"Hello, this is Henry West, landlord of 'The Lonely Shepherd'. I'd like to report..."

Henry stopped to consider just exactly what it was he was reporting. "Well, a murder I suppose... Yes, the landlord. Yes, that's right... No, I don't drink."

P.C John Fletcher and P.C Robert Moor were sitting in their car enjoying their kebabs when their meal was rudely interrupted by the car's two-way radio.

"Control to Sierra Oscar, are you receiving me? Come in Sierra Oscar"

The officers ignored it.

"Control to Sierra Oscar. Come in Sierra Oscar"

P.C Moor swallowed his kebab and thought for a while. "Isn't that us Fletch?"

"No, were Oscar Tango."

P.C Moor took another bite of his kebab.

"Control to Sierra Oscar. Are you receiving me Sierra Oscar?"

"Are you sure Fletch? I thought Steve and Deano were Oscar Tango."

"No, Steve and Deano are Sierra Oscar."

"Come in Sierra Oscar. Are you receiving me, Fletch?"

P.C Fletcher quickly picked up the handset (much to the amusement of his partner).

"Sierra Oscar receiving."

"Fletch, we've had a report from the landlord of 'The Lonely Shepherd'. Where exactly are you by the way?"

We're outside the service station on Collingworth Road. What's wrong? Over."

"Probably nothing. A Ford Mustang left, 'The Lonely Shepherd' about five minutes ago; it should be heading your way. The sarge would like you to do a drive by, just get its registration number and see if you can spot anything suspicious. Over"

"Ok June, got that."

P.C Fletcher replaced the handset just as the Ford Mustang passed the petrol station.

Back at the station, June sat at the control desk and waited. Sergeant Beck paced up and down behind her.

"Probably nothing Sarge," said June.

Sergeant Beck paced some more.

"Could be a crank."

Sergeant Beck stopped pacing, took off his hat and rubbed his head. "I don't know, June. I could understand it if someone had rung in to say they'd seen three men taking a spade and a body out of a boot and heading off on to the moors." He seemed to come to a decision and stopped rubbing his head. "I'm going to inform the Super. Get on to the Fast Action Response Team and put them on alert."

"You want me to ring the FART squad sir? Hadn't we better wait for Fletch to call in?"

Sergeant Beck replaced his hat. "No, I want to get things in motion on this one. And June, don't let me hear you referring to the F.A.R team by that acronym again. You've read the memo."

June had indeed read the memo. "Sorry, Sarge."

June made a few phone calls and monitored the radio for a short while until Sergeant Beck returned with the station's Superintendent.

"Right June," said Sergeant Beck, "any news?"

"No Sarge, still waiting for Fletch to report."

"Did you contact the Fast Action Response Team?"

"I gave the Fart squad a ring a couple of minutes ago and..."

June's sentence was cut short by a sharp look from her Sergeant. Superintendent Thompson lowered the clipboard from which he had been reading the basic outline of events so far. "W.P.C Taylor, isn't it?"

"Yes Sir."

"Well, W.P.C Taylor, I'm going to take it you haven't yet seen the memo from the Chief Constable of Greater Manchester."

"No Sir."

"Then let me outline it for you. Basically, it is to do with the lack of respect and professionalism of some officers regarding the F.A.R.T. it warns of disciplinary action against any officer showing disrespect for fellow officers. Am I making myself clear?"

"Yes Sir."

"Good. Because had you read the memo, I would have had to conclude that not only had I an officer under my command who was prepared to show a lack of respect for her fellow officers, but who was also prepared to disobey a direct order from the Chief Constable of Greater Manchester! The memo points out W.P.C Taylor, that the Fast Action Response Team is a dedicated group of men and women highly trained and on standby 24 hours a day, ready to react to any situation at a moment's notice, and I will not have them ridiculed by officers under my command, is that clear?"

"Yes Sir."

"Good. Now what did the Fast Action Response Team say?"

"Well sir," June looked at Sergeant Beck as if she needed support and then lowered her head again. "They're not answering the phone at the moment."

The awkward silence that followed was interrupted by a voice on the radio.

"Sierra Oscar to control."

June was glad of the chance to return to her desk. "Go ahead, Sierra Oscar."

"We have pulled up at the traffic lights behind the suspect vehicle. There are three men inside and the registration plate is Yankee Whisky..." there was a moments silence as Fletch hit a problem *"... L, one, zero, five."*

June looked at Sergeant Beck who in return looked embarrassed.

"Is that L for Lima, Sierra Oscar?"

"Oh, that's right June, I always forget that one. Lima, one, zero, five Tango and June..."

"Yes, Sierra Oscar, what is it?"

"There appears to be blood on the back number plate."

June turned to her senior officers.

"Right," said the Superintendent. "Er... tell them to fall back but maintain visual contact. I'll be in my office... and try to get on to the Fart squad again!"

"Stop panicking," said Taffy. "There's no one following I tell you."

Lenny turned away from the rear window he had been gazing through for the last couple of miles. "Maybe you're right, but I'm sure it was a Police car that pulled behind us at that last set of lights. How's the hand?"

Taffy lifted his hand to display the damage. "I'd say that was broken, wouldn't you Numbnuts?"

Numbnuts took his eye from the road for a second. "Sorry Taff."

"You'll have to go to hospital with that," stated Lenny sympathetically.

"I'll go in the morning."

"I'll take you if you like, Taff."

"Oh thanks, that's very fuckin' civil of you that is. Thank you for that, thanks a fuckin' lot!"

Numbnuts understood Taffy's sarcasm and decided to remain silent and just concentrate on the road.

"Stop looking through that window. I've told you no one is bothered about one poxy sheep."

"There's a van behind us," reported Lenny.

Lenny's paranoia was beginning to get on Taffy's nerves. "It's probably the sheep police. You watch, any minute now a police helicopter will land in front of us and Starsky an' fuckin' Hutch'll jump out."

Taffy's comments had done their job; Lenny felt silly and once again turned away from the window.

"How much is a sheep worth then Taffy?"

"Well, once it's cut up," Taffy paused for a moment to consider the question a little more fully. "Well, work it out; you've got lamb of course, about half a pound of lamb's liver. You've got a couple of dozen lamp chops, two legs of lamb, and if we can get hold of a mincer, we'll have a couple of pounds of mince. We should clear £8 a carcass."

"£8?" Lenny seemed a little disappointed. "£8, that's not much."

"No, but don't forget this is just a practice run, next time we'll come back with half a dozen. That's six times £8, that's... well, it's a bob or two."

"Four," said Numbnuts.

Taffy seemed bewildered. "Four? Six times eight is four?"

"No four legs. A sheep has four legs."

"Thank you, David Attenborough," interjected Lenny as he leaned forward, "but we already knew that."

"Yes, but Taffy said two legs of lamb."

"That's because you only use the back legs for leg of lamb," said Taffy.

"Ah, I didn't know that."

Numbnuts went back to concentrating on driving. Taffy was trying to work out what six times eight came to and Lenny was thinking of a pink bicycle, when the white transit decided to overtake. The van pulled smoothly in front, but then, for no apparent reason, began to slow down.

"Aye up," said Numbnuts. "What's he up to?"

"Just overtake him," suggested Taffy.

"I can't. I can't see. This if left hand drive you know."

The transit van came to a halt and so did Sally. Suddenly, the back doors flew open, and a blinding spotlight engulfed them. There was the sound of shouting and running feet. Numbnuts and Taffy were showered with broken glass as Sally's side windows were smashed. The screaming voices were clearer now.

"ARMED POLICE. GET OUT OF THE CAR!"

Numbnuts, Taffy and Lenny had little choice; they were being manhandled by group of officers. The light from the back of the van was still blinding, but for a second Taffy caught sight of one of the officers. He was wearing a bulletproof vest and carrying a gun. There were large white letters across his chest that read 'POLICE F.A.R.T.' Taffy attempted to take a second look before he was forced to the floor. With his cheek against the tarmac and a torch in his face. Taffy saw very little of what was going on around him until a second face hit the tarmac and was illuminated by a second torch a few feet away. Lenny's eyes were closed, and his face screwed up in pain as his arms were forced farther up his back rather more than nature had intended. Eventually, Lenny felt the click of handcuffs around his wrists and his arms were released. Lenny's face straightened and his eyes opened to the sight of Taffy who was trying to force a smile.

"Alright?"

Lenny declined to answer.

"They don't half take sheep rustling seriously round here don't they."

Once again, Lenny declined to answer.

Sergeant Smith was in charge of the Fast Action Response Team that night and it was he who made the radio call back to base from a radio on his lapel.

"Target secure."

Sergeant Smith made his way over to Sally and examined the boot before turning to one of his junior officers.

"Right, let's have this thing opened."

The junior officer ran off towards the transit van and returned with a large crowbar. After forcing the end of the crowbar in the gap at the base of the boot, he awaited the order from Sergeant Smith. Sergeant Smith nodded at two of his officers who raised their rifles and pointed them at the boot, then he signalled for the boot to be opened. The top sprang open and out leapt a young sheep, which, although a little unsteady on its feet, managed to make its way up the road and disappear into darkness.

"Is that it?" asked one of the officers.

Sergeant Smith looked confused. He searched the boot and found nothing but a spade.

"You're telling me, we've been dragged out here for a couple of sheep rustlers. We'll be a laughing stock," announced another officer.

"Right," said Sergeant Smith. "You go and get that sheep."

One of the officers grudgingly set off up the road, unsure whether or not his Sergeant was joking.

"Quickly, its evidence."

"We're not going to arrest a couple of rustlers are we Sarge? We're going to look daft.

"Not as daft as we'll look going back without an arrest. Besides, it's a very serious offence, sheep rustling. Get those three into van."

Lenny, Numbnuts and Taffy were forced into the van and the door was slammed shut.

The chief magistrate carefully examined the list of previous convictions.

Leonard Grey 1979 Behaviour likely to cause a breach of peace.
1980 Breach of the peace.

Daniel Winston Harrison No previous convictions.
Jonathon Owen 1972 Drunk and Disorderly.
1974 Drunk and Disorderly.
1974 Public Indecency and Drunk and Disorderly.
1980 Drunk and Disorderly.

"Well, there doesn't appear to be any past history of dishonesty." The chief magistrate passed the sheet of previous convictions to his colleagues for confirmation. "I suggest a stern dressing down and a suspended sentence."

The other two magistrates agreed.

"Will the defendants please rise."

Lenny, Taffy and Numbnuts rose, and the chief magistrate put on his glasses.

"You have pleaded guilty to theft and cruelty to livestock under section sixteen of the cruelty to animal act of 1976. Do you have anything to say before sentence is passed?"

Numbnuts and Taffy looked at Lenny and sat back down. This was the moment they had been waiting for.

After Taffy had returned from hospital (with his hand in plaster) they had sat up in their cell for most of the night discussing their plight and had decided their best course of action was to plead poverty due to the strike and throw themselves at the mercy of the court. It had been decided that Lenny should be the spokesperson after it had been agreed that Taffy's accent may be a draw back. Numbnuts wasn't considered to be a viable option.

Lenny had gone over his speech many times in his head editing and re-editing, until he felt it good enough to melt the heartstrings of any reasonable human being. He had planned to mention the year long strike in which they had received no government benefits, his wife and daughter, and his *piece de resistance:* his inability to put food on the table for them at Christmas. Lenny cleared his throat.

"Your honour, you see before you three men with families. Three proud men who have always been able to provide for those families, until earlier this year when the means for them to provide was taken away from them, from us," Lenny corrected, "with the threat of closure to their colliery. To prevent that happening they decided to go on strike, to do without. Now a man can do without most things in life, but he cannot do without the basics, food, water and shelter. Food your honour, a basic necessity..."

"Then go back to work."

The chief magistrate's interjection had taken Lenny completely by surprise. This was something he hadn't expected.

"Sorry?"

"Mr Grey," said the chief magistrate, "I hope you are not going to waste the court's time with some long-winded speech about poverty leading to crime. I see people all the time who are out of work and living below the poverty line and I do have sympathy with such people. Those people, however, quite often have no choice in the matter; they are quite often unable to get employment. You three have employment, employment that has served you well over the years and yet you choose not to take advantage of that employment. Quite frankly, if you wish to provide for your families, you should go back to work to earn your basic necessities, as you put it, instead of stealing them from others."

The chief magistrate took off his glasses again and began to review some case notes. "If there's nothing further," he added without looking up from his notes.

Lenny sat back down. His disappointment began to turn to anger as what the magistrate had said to him began to sink in. He decided he wasn't prepared to let this insult to him, and thousands like him go unchallenged. He began to rise but then noticed Taffy had beaten him to it.

"That's not what he was going to say."

The chief magistrate sat back in his chair and began to chew the end of his glasses. "Really, what is it then?

"He was going to say…" He, like Lenny felt he had something to say, the trouble was he didn't know what. He had to return the insult, then it came to him, and he smiled. "We fail to recognise this court."

The glasses fell from the magistrate's mouth as his jaw dropped. One of the other magistrates pressed too hard on his note pad and broke his pencil and the court stenographer stopped typing and looked up as if she was unsure, she had heard correctly. Even exhibit A, a young sheep with a bandage on his head, bleated out its disapproval as it looked up at the W.P.C who was holding its lead.

Taffy thought he might have gone too far, and his courage began to desert him. Lenny sank his head into his hands as if he wanted to hide. The courtroom was silent, and everyone was staring at Taffy. He had gone too far. The I.R.A mainland bombing case was no laughing matter as far as the courts were concerned. Taffy's courage fled by the back door, and he stood alone.

"Well," said Taffy nervously, "it's been decorated since the last time we were here."

Chapter Six

Charlie Marshall

"That's it," said a voice from the kitchen. "I've had it just about up to here."

Janet entered the room with her hand on her forehead. "Men! You try to please them, cook and clean, you spend more than you should on brisket, you make yourself look nice..." Janet stopped suddenly as she looked at Sue for the first time since her arrival. "Luvvy, what's a matter?" Janet sat beside Sue on the sofa and took her by the hand. "What are you crying for? What's happened?"

Sue wiped her eyes. "It's nothing. I've been up all night, that's all."

"Why have you been up all night? What's gone off? Where's your Lenny?"

Sue began to cry again so Janet put her arm around her.

"He's in prison."

"What?" Janet was quite shocked at the news. "What 'as he been doing?"

"I don't know exactly." Sue wiped her eyes once more. "He didn't come home last night, then I got a phone call at about nine this morning from a Sergeant Beck saying he was in police custody, and he was due in court at ten o'clock. Then Sandra rings me up at about half past twelve and tells me they've been sentenced to fourteen days for contempt of court."

"What, Sandra's Numbnuts? 'As he got time an'all?"

Sue nodded. "And Taffy."

Janet looked annoyed. "Taffy Owen! I might have known he'd have something to do with it." Janet thought for a while. "Fourteen days... that'll be Christmas Eve."

"What?" Sue had completely forgotten about Christmas.

"That means they'll be out for Christmas. Wonder what they've been up to?"

Sue seemed to have pulled herself together, so Janet removed her arm.

"I don't know, some harebrained scheme, knowing Lenny. He's always up to something. It's this bloody strike; he just feels he's letting us down all the time, but he's not, we're managing." Sue paused for a while. "It's probably about the bike."

"What bike?" asked Janet curiously.

"Our Lisa wants a bike for Christmas, and he got himself all worked up last night over it. The thing is, I've been saving coupons and I've just about got enough to get her a bloody bike."

"And he didn't know that?"

"No, I didn't want to get his or Lisa's hopes up in case I don't manage it in time for Christmas."

"Are they Tesco coupons?" Sue nodded. Janet smiled and reached for her shopping bag. "Here, these have been cluttering up in my bag for weeks." Janet handed over a handful of Tesco coupons.

"I couldn't."

"Go on, they're no good to me. I do most my shopping at Quicksave. I'll never save enough of the damned things to get anything worthwhile anyway."

Sue smiled for the first time that morning. "Thanks Janet."

Janet for some reason felt a little embarrassed and decided to change the subject.

"What night did you say that thing was on?"

"What thing?"

"You know, that thing at the community centre, for people with… problems."

"Oh, you've talked him into going then."

"No, but I'm going to go. I think you were right. It may do me good just to hear other people have the same problems."

Sue thought for a while. "Well, last night was mothers-to-be night. I know that because Tracey Evans goes. Friday is the people who want to give up smoking, or at least it was when I went. It may be tonight or Thursday. I don't know Janet; there's a lot of people use the community centre. You'll just have to go along and ask."

"Hey, they might have a prisoner's wife support group, shall I ask?" Janet gave Sue a little laugh and Sue smiled back.

"Silly bugger, go and put kettle on."

Lenny, Taffy and Numbnuts sat quietly in what appeared to be a classroom. The blackboard in front of them had one name on it: Mr Wilson. Lenny wondered who Mr Wilson was. He also wondered who the other two inmates occupying separate tables by the window were. Lenny had thought it was reasonable to assume them to be inmates as they were wearing the same light blue shirts and dark blue trousers as himself, Numbnuts and Taffy. The door opened and in walked a prison guard carrying a large black folder. The guard walked around the classroom and handed out two pieces of A4 paper to each of the inmates before standing by the blackboard at the front of the room.

"I'm Mr Wilson (Mr Wilson pointed at the blackboard) and I'm your prison welfare officer. It's my job to deal with any problems you may have settling into prison life." Mr Wilson opened his folder and studied it for a while. "I see you're all short termers. Right, if you look at the two sheets of paper I have given you, on one of them you will find a list of prison rules. On section two of that list, under drugs and banned substances, you will find a list. If any of you are taking any of these, either under prescription or not, I need to know so I can make you an appointment with the prison doctor."

Mr Wilson looked up briefly, but there was no response. "Good. Anyway, I would appreciate it if tonight in your cells you would take time to read through the rules. A great many of them are there for your own safety. The other piece of paper is an itinerary; it will tell you the times of the various classes available, lunch times, tea times, lights out, that sort of thing. At number six of the sports section, you will see athletics." Lenny scanned the list and found the line that read *Athletics... South sports field, 2pm-4pm. Saturdays... Mr Wilson.* Anyone interested in athletics?"

Mr Wilson again looked up and again found no response. "Pity," he continued, "I usually get some interest, even if it is mostly in the pole-vault." Mr Wilson beamed a smile, but again, got no response. "Anyway, if I can help you with any of the courses, please let me know. The other thing I may be able to help you with is your families; if they are having any problems, let me know. I might be able to speak to Social Services and get them the necessary support. Any questions? No? Right then, it's twenty-to-twelve, I'll let you go and get your dinner."

Mr Wilson gathered up his papers, placed them into his folder and left; he was closely followed by one of the inmates. The other left his table by the window and joined Lenny, Taffy and Numbnuts, who seemed to ignore his approach. Lenny was busy reading the itinerary schedule, Numbnuts was reading the rules and Taffy was busy making a paper aeroplane.

"Hi. I'm Norman."

Lenny stopped reading. "I'm Lenny, this is Danny and that's Taffy."

Norman nodded his head, "first time?"

"Yeah," said Numbnuts. "Yours?"

"Fifth."

"Fifth time in the slammer! Ah, you must be one mean mother fucker."

Lenny and Numbnuts wondered why Taffy was trying (unsuccessfully) to fake an American accent.

"Not really," said Norman who also seemed to be pondering Taffy's accent.

"What are you in for?" asked Numbnuts curiously.

"Non-payment of fines."

"What, they lock you up for non-payment of fines?"

"Yes, but it's ok; it's easier than paying."

Lenny looked puzzled so Norman went on to explain, "I was fined a few years ago and never paid it, so they took me back to court and fined me some more. When I didn't pay that, they put me in prison. And that's how it's been for the last three or four years. They let me out for a couple of months, I don't pay, they put me back in."

"That's pathetic," proclaimed Lenny.

"Tell me about it, but like I say, it's ok; I've got used to it."

"Why don't you pay the fine?"

"I wish I could, but what chance have I? I haven't got a job and I'm not likely to get one; by the time I get to an interview they've thrown me back inside." Norman shrugged his shoulder. "Anyway, what you in for?"

Lenny threw a dirty look Taffy's way. "It's a long story."

The classroom door opened, and a prison officer popped his head in. "Mr Wilson gone, has he?" The four men indicated that he had. "Well, come on then let's have you; you can't stay in here unaccompanied."

Lenny, Numbnuts, Taffy and Norman left the room and a few minutes later found themselves sitting down for dinner in a large dining room. Prison so far hadn't been quite what they had expected. The dining room for instance wasn't at all how Numbnuts had pictured it. Behind the serving area was a menu board offering braising steak and mash with two veg, or sausage, chips and beans. There was also a vegetarian menu offering a vegetarian lasagne. Lenny, Numbnuts, Taffy and Norman made their choice and scanned the room for an empty table. One was spotted by one of the tiled pillars that supported the huge, doomed roof, thirty feet above. The four men sat down and began their meal.

"Well," said Numbnuts, "It's not what I expected."

"Really?" Norman struggled to cut his braising steak with his plastic knife. "What did you expect?"

"I don't know. I saw a film once where all the prisoners sat at a long wooden table and weren't allowed to talk or anything, and they didn't have food like this." Numbnuts shovelled in some mashed potato. "Porridge I think they had. There was this one prisoner that asked one of the guards for some more and was beaten for it." Numbnuts took another fork full then paused for a moment as if something had just occurred to him "or was that Oliver Twist?"

"It may look okay on the surface, but there are some really bad people in here,"

Norman looked around the room for a moment. "See him there," he pointed to a thick-set man with a bald head about four tables away. "That's William Moody aka Billy the axe. Chopped his neighbours up for having their TV on too loud."

"What did he do with the stiffs?" asked Taffy who was still trying to talk like an American gangster."

"What do you mean?"

"Well, when you make a hit on someone, you usually hide the stiff, every punk knows that."

Lenny looked puzzled. "Why are you talking like Marlon Brando?"

Taffy leaned across the table and lowered his voice. "When you're in a place like this its best to walk the walk and talk the talk." Taffy tapped his nose and winked.

Numbnuts shook his head. "What the fuck's he talking about?"

"I haven't got a clue."

"Listen," whispered Taffy, dropping the accent for the first time. "We don't want to appear weak; we need to be accepted, so, we walk the walk and talk the talk."

Lenny shook his head. "You really are a prick, aren't you?"

Numbnuts was the first to finish his meal. He sat back in his chair and asked, "What was he on about, people like doing the pole-vault?"

Numbnuts' question was directed at Lenny, but Lenny did not respond. Instead, he sat staring at one of his prisoners at a nearby table.

"What's up?"

"That bloke over there, isn't that..." Lenny stopped as if deep in thought.

"Charlie Marshall," said Norman. "Do you know him?"

"No, only what I've seen on the telly."

"Who's Charlie Marshall?" asked Numbnuts as he turned to see what everyone was looking at.

"Charlie Marshall is not a very popular person," Norman said frankly.

"Why? What's he done?"

"Charlie Marshall is doing five years in here for armed robbery whilst the rest of the gang are in Wormwood scrubs doing thirty!"

"How come?"

"He cut a deal with the police and grassed them up. That's why he's not very popular."

Numbnuts took a sip of his tea and Norman and Taffy went back to their dinners.

Lenny sat quietly. He was still staring at Charlie Marshall. It had always puzzled Lenny why a man would steal a million pounds and then turn himself in.

Janet stepped off the number 47 bus across the road from the Edward Dunn Community Centre and took a deep breath. 'Well girl', she told herself, 'This is it'. She crossed the road with a determined walk and reached out to open the double glass doors leading to the community centre foyer. Then she froze.

"Hello Janet," said a voice.

Janet turned to see a large figure walking towards her. Janet strained her eyes against the dimness of a December evening. As the figure got closer, light from the foyer fell upon its face.

"Hello Levi, gave me a bit of a fright there."

Levi was used to giving people frights and apologised. "Sorry, but have you heard about Lenny?"

"What?" Janet wondered how much to tell him. She wasn't sure about gossiping about her best friend's husband. She didn't think Sue would appreciate it.

"Him, Taffy and Numbnuts have all got time, so Liz Fisher's been saying."

"Yes, I heard that, yes," Janet relented a little. If Liz Fisher knew, Janet thought, everyone was going to find out anyway.

"Well?" asked Levi.

"Well, what?"

"Well, what have they been up to?"

"I don't really know," Janet admitted. "Something about contempt of court."

"Yeah, that's what Liz said, but she didn't know why they were in court in the first place."

"What," Janet said sarcastically, "there's something that Liz Fisher dunt know?"

"What?"

"Nothing." Janet had an idea. "I think Taffy was up for a burgling an old pensioner and Lenny and Numbnuts were there as witnesses, and they had some sort of argument with the judge." Janet found it hard to keep from smiling. She had just started a rumour slandering Taffy Owen (someone she didn't care much for) and she knew that it would get back to Liz who would spread it round the village and therefore, get the blame.

"Never!" Levi seemed shocked. "I know money's tight, but I wouldn't have thought that of Taffy."

"Well, it's only what I've heard."

"Who told you that?"

"Let's just say Liz confides in me a little more than she does in you. Anyway, talking of hard times, I hear you've got a job."

"Oh, yes, err, that's right."

"What are you doing?"

"Well, it's, it's sort of a collection and err, stuff."

Janet couldn't help feeling that Levi was being evasive, almost embarrassed even, so, she pressed on. "What kind of stuff?"

"Listen," said Levi. "I've got to go." With that, set off up the road turning briefly to call back, "Give my regards to Sue and Sandra."

"Ok Levi, see you."

Janet forgot Levi's peculiar reaction the minute she entered the foyer of the Edward Dunn Community Centre; she had other things on her mind. After browsing through some of the leaflets that had spread about on the coffee table, Janet was starting to wonder if this was such a good idea.

The main doors opened, and a middle-aged man entered. He was wearing a tweed jacket, sporting a large white kipper tie, and was carrying a briefcase, which made him appear to Janet to have some sort of official capacity. This man smiled at her and set off towards the staircase that led to the conference rooms on the second floor. As he reached the foot of the stairs, he stopped and turned back.

"Can I help you with something?" he asked politely.

"I don't really know. I'm looking for one of the support groups actually."

"Really. Which one?"

Janet didn't fancy having this conversation over the length of the foyer and joined the man at the foot of the stairs.

"I'm looking for the group," said Janet nervously, "that deals with people with problems." The man gestured with his body language for more information. "Of a personal nature," she added.

The man smiled. "I'm on my way up there now. I'm Mike and I take that group."

Mike held his hand out and Janet took it, "I'm Janet Mul..."

Mike cut Janet short by raising his hands. "Please, we don't do second names."

"Right," said Janet who was quite pleased at the first name only idea. "Well, I was wondering what I do to join."

"You don't. It's very informal and confidential. We have no members as such. We meet every Thursday and people... well, its up to the individual. Some come for reassurance, you know, to know that there are other people with the same problems, some just need to talk."

"That's me," interjected Janet. "I just need to talk to someone. It's my husband, you see."

Once more Mike raised his hands. "Not here; in group." Mike smiled a reassuring smile. "Come on, meet the group." He set off up the stairs.

Janet called after him. "What? Now?"

Mike stopped and once more faced Janet. "Unless you want to pop back some other time."

Janet thought for a moment and then set off up the stairs. "What the hell!"

Mike and Janet entered the conference room to find a group of five others waiting patiently.

"Good evening group," Mike bidded.

"Good evening, Mike," bid the group.

Mike retrieved two chairs from the back of the room and arranged them to complete a circle that had been partially formed by the rest of the group. When he and Janet were seated, Mike opened his suitcase and took out a notepad and pen.

"Ok everyone, this is Janet."

"Hello Janet," bid the group.

"Janet, would you like to tell the group something about yourself?"

"Well, my name is Janet um…" Janet remembered what Mike had said about surnamed and began again. "My name is Janet and I've come here… well you know, because I really am getting desperate."

"What do you mean, getting desperate?" asked Mike.

"Well, you know, I haven't had…" Janet who had never been the shy type was finding this more difficult than she had anticipated. "I haven't had…any…for seven months now, and I'm getting really desperate."

"I see," said Mike with his usual reassuring smile that was beginning to get on Janet's nerves. "Would it help you to know that Miriam here hasn't had anything for over a year." Mike was indicating one of the two women in the group who was smiling an embarrassed smile.

"Poor love," said Janet. "Well, Miriam will know what I mean then. Its hard int it Miriam?"

Miriam nodded in agreement. "And have you tried anything over the last seven months to help you get through?"

"I have masturbated if that's what you mean." Janet noted a snigger from one of the men in the group. "What? You think only men have a wank?"

Mike looked a little shocked. "And this has helped?"

"Well, it has, but it's getting to be a habit." Now two of the men and one of the women were giggling. "Well, it does, dunt it Miriam? I mean, I never used to do it at all, but when you're not getting the real thing, you have to make do."

"So, you're not having regular sex?"

"I'm not having any chuffin' sex, I've told you, not for seven months."

Now, with the exception of Mike, everyone was sniggering.

"So, you stopped having sex about the same time you realised you were an alcoholic?"

"Who's a bloody alcoholic?"

Mike looked puzzled. "Well… we are."

Janet's face coloured up as the realisation of her situation sank in. "So, this is a group for people with drink problems?"

Mike nodded.

"I've come to the wrong group."

Mike nodded again.

Janet rose from her chair gracefully, “I think I better go.”

Janet walked to the door and the laughter got louder. As she opened the door, she stopped for a moment and without turning around spoke. “I'm sorry I have wasted everyone's time.” The laughter was intense now. “I'll have to go now… I think I'll go and have a fuckin' good drink!”

Janet closed the door behind her and smiled to herself as the laughter subsided.

The prison bell rang at 8pm, as Lenny knew it would; he had read about it in the prison timetable. Nevertheless, it still came as a shock. He looked up at Numbnuts and Taffy who stared back in silence. Their first day in prison had been interesting to say the least and not at all what they had expected. Lenny had visited Mr. Wilson after dinner and had been supplied with a prison phone card worth £1. Lenny had used 30p worth of credits phoning home in a fruitless effort to stop Sue visiting him on the following Saturday. It wasn't that he didn't want to see his wife, it was just that he didn't want his wife to see him, not here, in prison. Lenny had also taken a trip to the prison library, made himself a member, drawn out two books. Now, with the sounding of the bell, everyone as packing whatever they were doing and making their way back to a ten-by-eight cell to be locked in for the night.

“Well!” said Taffy. “I'll see youse guys in the morning.”

Lenny and Numbnuts were sharing a cell (Cell 14, corridor D, West wing). Taffy had been given cell 24A, also on West wing, but he was sharing with someone called Nick Green. Taffy hadn't yet met Nick Green, but he had noticed Nick Green's name on the chalkboard outside the cell.

“Yeah, see you in the morning,” said Numbnuts.

Taffy hung his cue on the rack beside the pool table and left.

“Come on you two, you've heard the bell,” bellowed one of the guards.

Lenny and Numbnuts replaced their cues in the rack and made their way silently back to their cell.

The door to cell 14D had been left open during the day, under rule 66 on Lenny's sheet. Lenny and Numbnuts entered and sat on their beds on opposite sides of the room. A coffee table occupied the back wall, separating the two beds, and a sink and mirror hung on the front wall by the steel door. The coffee table seemed to Lenny to be an unusual piece of furniture for a prison cell, but on reflection he wondered if its presence was designed to make the cell look a little less like a cell. Numbnuts had wondered what time coffee would be served.

"Wonder how Taffy's getting on."

"He'll be alright," said Lenny, who happened to be wondering the same thing.

Taffy arrived at his cell to find the person he presumed to be Nick Green lying on his bed reading a body-building magazine. At first, it was hard for Taffy to understand why such a scrawny looking chap with lily-white skin and bleached blonde hair would have a passion for bodybuilding.

"Hi there," said Taffy throwing Nick a friendly smile.

Nick lowered his magazine and smiled back. "Well." Nick looked Taffy up and down.

"Hello to you," he replied in an extremely effeminate way.

Taffy's smile fell from his face and his words fell uncontrollably from his lips.

"Fuckin' hell."

"So, what happens now?" asked Numbnuts.

"Dunno. Just says lock up at 8 o'clock, lights out at 10." Lenny threw the timetable given to him by Mr. Wilson onto the coffee table and laid back on his bed.

"What are we supposed to do till ten?"

"I dunno." Lenny sat back up and retrieved one of the books he had taken out of the prison library. "I think I'll read."

Numbnuts sat for a short while then paced up and down for a short while before returning to sitting. "Fancy a game of cards?"

"Have you got any?"

Numbnuts remained silent, which told Leny that he had not. A few more minutes of silent sitting and pacing passed before Numbnuts spoke again. "What are you reading?"

Lenny looked at his book cover to remind him. "The dos and don'ts of creative writing."

"What?"

Lenny repeated himself.

"What's that about?"

"It's not about anything really. Its just full of tips on creative writing."

"What are you reading that for?"

"I was thinking of taking it up."

"What for?"

Lenny lowered his book and thought for a moment. "I don't really know, it's just something I always fancied. You know, leave my mark and all that." Lenny looked at the cell walls. "You know, Oscar Wilde wrote 'The Ballad of Reading Gaol' when he was in prison."

Numbnuts pretended for a moment to know what Lenny was on about before his curiosity got the better of him. "Who sang it?"

"Nobody sang it. It's a poem."

"What's it about?"

"Reading... jail. You know 'Iron bars do not a prison make nor four stone walls... a blah di blah di blah."

Numbnuts looked around at the four walls, then at the iron bars on the window and considered the words of Oscar Wilde. "Fat fucking lot he knew about prison then."

Lenny returned to his book.

"I've always wanted to play the guitar."

"Really," said Lenny in a disinterested way.

"Well, any instrument really."

"Uh huh."

"Sandra used to play the recorder when she was at school." Numbnuts picked up the itinerary sheet from the table. "Perhaps they do music lessons here."

"You're only gonna be here for a couple of weeks, you're hardly going to learn the guitar in that amount of time."

"I know. I was just thinking..." Numbnuts didn't have time to tell Lenny what he was thinking, he was interrupted by a prison officer entering the cell.

The officer quickly scanned the cell before referring to a register attached to his clipboard.

"Grey."

"Yeah."

The officer raised his eyes and looked at Lenny. "Number."

"5175"

The officer returned his gaze to the register. "Harrison."

"Yes."

"Number Harrison."

"Hold on, I've got it somewhere." Numbnuts searched his pockets.

"I wrote it down so I wouldn't forget it," he explained. "Oh yes, here it is." He produced a small piece of paper from his top pocket. "5176."

The guard made two ticks on his register before leaving. The large green metal door closed behind him, there was a metallic clicking sound followed by a final clink as the lock was operated.

Lenny and Numbnuts looked at each other; for the first time that day they really felt as if they were in prison.

"Nice breakfast," said Numbnuts as he shovelled in half a sausage dipped in beans. "You know, I don't eat this well at home."

Lenny nodded his head in agreement and went about his breakfast, preferring not to think of home.

"Mind if I join you?" said a familiar voice.

Numbnuts shuffled his chair to one side to allow Norman to access the table.

"How was your first night?" asked Norman as he seated himself and unloaded his tray. "Did you sleep well?"

"Eventually," said Lenny.

"It's a bit boring though," added Numbnuts.

"Yes, well, that's something you never get used to. Where's your mate?"

"Taffy," said Numbnuts. "Dunno, he's in a different cell to us. He'll be down in a bit I expect." Numbnuts shovelled in another half of sausage before continuing. "Ah Norman, there's something I've been meaning to ask you."

"Oh yes."

"Yes, I noticed some of the cells have got TV's."

"Yes."

"Well, how come we haven't got one?"

Norman began to butter his toast. "The TVs are given to the long termers as a privilege." Norman looked at Numbnuts and could see he didn't understand. "TVs are given to long-term prisoners as a privilege, that way the screws can revoke their privileges if they do anything wrong."

"I see, so we won't be getting a telly then."

"No, but there is a TV room. Aye up, your mates here."

Numbnuts waved at Taffy who was standing at the end of the serving area holding a tray and looking around the room. Numbnuts stood up and waved a little more aggressively until he caught Taffy's attention.

Taffy made his way over, unloaded his tray and pulled up a chair.

"Alright Taff?" asked Numbnuts politely.

"Yes, why shouldn't I be?"

Lenny was pleased to hear Taffy had lost his gangster accent but was a little concerned about the aggressive tone he seemed to have adopted. "Have a good night?" he asked.

"Yeah."

"Who are you in with?" asked Numbnuts.

Taffy looked around the table suspiciously. "Just a bloke."

"Alright, is he?"

"Yes, why?"

"Just wondered. You could have been sharing with Billy the axe for all we knew," interjected Lenny.

"Well, I'm not." Taffy started on his breakfast.

"Who are you sharing with?" asked Norman.

Taffy seemed a little embarrassed. "A bloke called Nick."

"Nick Green," said Norman laughing. "Arsenic."

"Yes."

"Who's arsenic?" asked Numbnuts. "Is he a murderer; did he poison someone?"

"No," laughed Norman.

"Then why do you call him arsenic?"

"Because he rents his arse out."

Numbnuts looked puzzled. "What do you mean he rents his arse out?"

Lenny was smiling like a Cheshire cat. "He means he's a male prostitute!"

"Fuck off," said Taffy without looking up from his plate.

"Well," said Lenny as he tried to contain his laughter. "Maybe the long cold nights won't be so long and cold."

Taffy slammed his teacup on the table, which caught the attention of some of the other prisoners who quickly went back to minding their own business.

Taffy spoke in an angry whisper. "I'm fuckin' telling you, don't start. If that little puff comes near me, I'll break his fuckin' neck."

"Ok, ok," said Lenny, who waited until Taffy had returned to his breakfast before adding, "no need to get arsey."

Breakfast finished by 9:30. Lenny and Taffy agreed to Numbnuts' request to go to the television room.

"But first," said Lenny. "I'm going to see that Mr. Wilson. I'll meet you there in half an hour."

Lenny left the dining room and after a couple of wrong turns into corridors blocked by iron bars, found himself outside Mr. Wilson's office. He knocked and a voice from within answered.

"Come in."

Lenny found Mr. Wilson sitting at his desk puzzling over his computer screen.

"Sit down," said Mr. Wilson.

Lenny did as he was bid.

"Do you know anything about computers?"

Lenny had to admit that he did not.

"Neither do I." Mr. Wilson turned away from the screen. "Right, what can I do for you?"

"Well," said Lenny. "I've been told that it's sometimes possible to...go home."

Mr. Wilson looked at Lenny with the same look he had given his computer. "Go home!"

"Yes, you know, home visits."

"You only came in yesterday."

"I know."

Mr. Wilson puzzled some more, but eventually agreed, "Yes, it's possible for some category prisoners to get supervised leave under certain circumstances if that's what you mean."

"That's what I want, supervised leave."

Mr. Wilson reluctantly turned to his computer. "Name?"

"Lenny Grey."

"Number?"

"5175"

Mr. Wilson typed the information into his computer and waited for Lenny's details to come up. "You're only in a fortnight."

"Yes, I know, but I've made arrangements."

"Most people in here had prior engagements."

"Yeah, but this is not for me… it's for the kids."

"This is the most unusual; tell me exactly what these prior arrangements are?"

"It's the school. My daughter's school."

"The school?"

"Yes, it hasn't got a Santa." Lenny thought for a moment. He wasn't making much sense. "It's me you see; I'm supposed to be the school Santa."

"Well, I'm afraid the school will have to get another Santa."

"No, you don't understand. The real Santa is an alcoholic and his kidneys have packed up." Lenny thought about what he had just said and decided to explain. "The bloke who usually does it is in hospital, and I've stepped in at the last minute. You see, I'm from a mining village and it's the kids, you see… there's not much money about and the kids are looking forward to it." Lenny sat back in his chair and looked dismayed. "God knows they haven't got much else to look forward to." Lenny looked up and saw that Mr. Wilson was quietly mulling things over in his head.

"Come on Mr. Wilson. It's not the kids' fault I'm in here."

This seemed to interrupt Mr. Wilson's mulling process and provoke a thought. He turned back to his computer. "What are you in for?"

"Arguing with a judge."

Mr. Wilson wasn't listening, he was punching up more details on his computer, "Contempt of court," he said as he turned back to Lenny and resumed mulling. "This is most unusual."

Lenny didn't answer. He waited for Mr. Wilson to come to a decision, which eventually, he did.

"I'll make you an appointment to see the governor."

"What does that mean?"

"Only the governor can grant supervised leave. It's entirely up to him, that's as much as I can do."

"Thank you," said Lenny excitedly.

"Don't get your hopes up, this is a very unusual request and as I say, it's up to the governor."

Lenny left with a final thank you and Mr. Wilson went back to his computer. "Most unusual... most unusual."

After his meeting with Mr. Wilson, Lenny made his way to the TV room. There he found Taffy and Numbnuts watching a documentary. Over in the corner of the room Lenny noticed something much more interesting.

Charlie Marshall was sitting at a table, across from an older man, who Lenny didn't recognise. The thing that interested Lenny was the wink he had received from Charlie on his arrival. Why, thought Lenny, would Charlie Marshall wink at him? It had come as such a surprise that Lenny decided to ignore it, but now as he sat himself down beside Numbnuts and Taffy he was finding it difficult to do so. Lenny looked back over his shoulder hoping to catch Charlie's eye, but to no avail Charlie was concentrating on his game.

"Alright?" said Numbnuts cheerfully.

"What you watching?" asked Lenny as he tried to occupy his mind with something other than Charlie's wink.

"It's a documentary on killer whales. Football's on at 1 o'clock."

"Who's playing?"

"Arsenal and Man City."

"That should be good." Lenny turned to look at Charlie once more.

"Did you know that killer whales have never been known to kill a human?" said Taffy.

"No, I err... I didn't know that." Lenny turned his attention back to the TV and once more tried to forget about Charlie. "Seems a bit daft calling them killer whales then really."

"That's what I said."

"They do kill seals though," interjected Numbnuts with a knowing nod of his head.

"One came rait up ont beach to get one, dint it, Taff?"

Taffy nodded in agreement. "Took the fat fucker about five minutes to get back into sea though."

Lenny turned to look at Charlie who was now shaking his partner's hand.

"They ought to call them seal killer whales really," suggested Numbnuts.

Charlie's partner left the room and Charlie began placing his chess pieces into a small wooden box.

"Yeah, but," said Taffy, "they do kill other things as well."

"Be back in a minute," said Lenny rising to his feet. He made his way over to Charlie's table and waited for Charlie to look up and notice him. Just as Lenny was beginning to think that Charlie wasn't going to notice him, he spoke.

"Do you play?"

Lenny had to look around to assure himself Charlie was addressing him, as Charlie's eyes hadn't yet left the board.

"Yes, I play."

Charlie looked up and smiled. "Do you want a game?"

"No."

"Then what do you want?"

"You winked at me when I came in."

"That's right."

"Why?"

Charlie shrugged his shoulders. "Just being neighbourly. We are neighbours, aren't we?"

Lenny was a little puzzled by this remark. "What do you mean?"

"You're the three guys from Molton aren't you?"

"That's right."

"Well, I live just over the hill in Brookly."

"I know."

"Then we're neighbours." Charlie clicked the top of the box shut.

"How do you know I'm from Molton?"

Charlie smiled. "You're in prison son, and people like to know who they're in prison with."

"I know who you are," said Lenny as if to impress. "You're Charlie Marshall the bloke who nicked a million."

"One point two million," admitted Charlie as he folded up the chessboard. "And you're Leonard Grey, the bloke who nicked a sheep!"

Lenny fell silent; he couldn't help but feel humiliated by Charlie's remark. He hadn't been rude or anything; what he said was true. It was the way he said it, as if he was in some way superior. Lenny couldn't quite put his finger on it, but he didn't like it.

Lenny sat down on the vacant seat and opened the board. "Let's play."

"Ooh it was awful," said Janet over the top of her coffee cup. "Everyone was laughing."

Sue was finding it hard not to laugh out loud herself. "So, when did you realise?"

"I didn't. God, Sue, you should have heard the things I was saying." Janet allowed herself a slight grin. "Then, this Mike asked me how long I'd been an alcoholic, that's when the penny dropped."

"Oh Janet. I feel so guilty."

"Guilty… why?"

"Well, it was me who encouraged you to go."

"It's not your fault silly chuff; it was me who got the wrong night."

"You're not going to try again then?"

"No, I think I'll give it up as a bad job."

The half time score was Man City 1, Arsenal 0 and Lenny and Charlie were well into their game. Numbnuts and Taffy had taken a short break from the football to see what Lenny was doing.

"Check mate in three moves," Taffy whispered to Numbnuts.

Numbnuts looked impressed. "I dint know you could play chess. I knew Lenny could; he was the best in our school."

"Yes, I once played against Bobby Fisher," whispered Taffy from behind his hand.

"Lenny'll have him in check mate in three moves, you watch."

Numbnuts studied the board for a moment. "How?"

"He takes Lenny's horsey with his castle, Lenny takes his castle with his prawn, he takes Lenny's prawn with his prawn, Leny calls check with his castle, he brings his long thin one out to protect his king, and Lenny takes his long thin one with his queen: Check mate!"

Charlie moved his rook across the board and ignored Lenny's horsey. "Check."

"Wrong move," said Taffy and went back to the football. Numbnuts watched Lenny advance his bishop before following Taffy.

Charlie smiled and took Lenny's pawn from the board with his knight. "I don't think your mind's on this game." Charlie was right; Lenny was finding it hard to concentrate even though he desperately wanted to beat Charlie.

"What's bothering you?" asked Charlie.

"Nothing." Lenny advanced his bishop. Charlie studied the move carefully. "It's the robbery," said Lenny. "Why did you just turn yourself in?"

Charlie sat back in his chair as if he was considering something. "Causality. You know, probable outcomes." Charlie's words came out very slowly as if they had been plucked with extra care from his vocabulary.

"What do you mean? You got clean away with a million pounds then you went and handed yourself in! I don't get it. Never did."

Charlie considered some more. "Nobody gets clean away with a million pounds."

Lenny looked puzzled. "As I said, it's all to do with probable outcomes, like chess. Yes, that's it, it's like chess."

Lenny sat quietly contemplating Charlie's words.

"Your king's bishop," said Charlie. "What would you do if I took it with my knight?" Lenny was hoping Charlie was going to take his bishop and so didn't answer. "I'm not going to take the bishop," said Charlie.

"I would have called check with my rook."

"And I would have had to move my king, leaving my queen vulnerable."

"And I would have taken your queen; you would have taken my rook."

"So," said Charlie. "The probable outcome would be for me to capture your rook and bishop, but I would lose my queen, and you should never loose your queen. Now, what is the probable outcome for someone who steals one point two million pounds?"

"I don't know. A life of luxury I suppose."

"Wrong," said Charlie. "The probable outcome for someone who steals a hundred grand is life of luxury; people steal a hundred grand every day. The police ask a few questions then file and shelve the case. The probable outcome for someone who nicks one point two million pounds is twenty-five years minimum. The police never give up on that amount – ask the Great Train Robbers." Charlie advanced his queen's bishop.

Lenny took Charlie's pawn with one of his own. "Ronny Biggs got away."

"Ronny Biggs spent most of his money getting out the country; he's skint. Buster Edwards hated it so much he came back and was sent to jail with the rest of them." Charlie advanced a knight.

Lenny responded by advancing his own knight. "If that's the case, why did you steal the money in the first place?"

Charlie shook his head as if he had asked himself the same question many times before. "There wasn't supposed to be that much. The armoured car we robbed carried used notes from all the Sheffield banks to Manchester for burning."

"For what?"

"Burning. That's what they do with old notes, they burn them. Anyway, we knew that about five percent of bank notes were burnt every week. We knew how many banks were in Sheffield and we estimated the van would be carrying about a hundred grand, but we must have messed up on the decimal point or something. There was nobody more surprised than us when we heard on the radio later that afternoon how much had been stolen."

"You heard on the radio! You mean you never counted it or anything?"

"No, we stashed the money, and we were going to lay low for a couple of weeks, at least that was the plan. Check."

"So," said Lenny as he blocked Charlie's move with his knight. "You decided to turn yourself in."

"It was a case of doing that and cutting a deal or going on the run, getting caught and spending the rest of my days behind bars,"

"So," said Lenny, "what happened to the money?"

Charlie took Lenny's knight from the board with his queen and smiled. "I don't know. I gave my share back." Charlie waved his queen in front of Lenny before placing it on the square that had been occupied by Lenny's knight. "Like I said, you should never give up your queen. Check and mate."

Colin sat on the dry-stone wall, in front of the pier that stretched out into the icy waters of the boating lake. The moonlight illuminated the rickety old pier, but after that he could see nothing but darkness. It was a darkness that seemed to beckon Colin into taking a few short steps along the pier and disappear into it.

Not that Colin needed beckoning. He had already made his mind up that this was what he would do and this time there would be no mistakes.

Colin picked up his rucksack, pulled out a length of chain and placed it in his lap. Then, out of the zip pocket, Colin produced an envelope containing a letter.

Colin had sat at his bedside table for over an hour trying to find the words he wanted to say. But what could he say? His mother would never understand, and even if she did, she would soon forget. Colin read the letter one last time.

Sorry mum, I've gone to see dad. I hope you can forgive me. It's for the best. Colin.

Colin had brought a pen with him, hoping for some sort of inspiration, some way of explaining things a little better, but Colin was feeling far from inspired.

He slipped the letter back into the zip pocket and pulled out two padlocks, a crowbar and a bunch of keys. Colin had come well prepared; this time there would be no mistakes. He was aware that it was almost impossible for someone to drown himself if they could swim. It was impossible to sink to the bottom of an ice-cold lake and just run out of air without instinct kicking in. Colin had decided there would be none of that; this time he would do it right.

Colin forced the crowbar into the dry-stone wall and eased free one of the larger stones from its base. After wrapping one end of the chain around it and securing it with one of the padlocks. Colin fastened the other end around his own wrist, securing that with the second padlock. He looked out over the lake. That was it, he thought, nothing left to chance... except. Colin looked down and opened his hand. The padlock keys glittered in the moonlight. He threw the keys over his shoulder and set off along the pier. Every step Colin took made the pier creak and groan. The added weight of the stone and chain he was struggling to carry worried him. He felt as if the pier was about to give way at any moment. Not that he was worried abut going straight through it and drowning – that would be fine. What was worrying Colin was going halfway through and then getting stuck. It was all a little more difficult than he had anticipated and the pot on his foot wasn't helping things. Colin pressed on. Eventually he reached the very end of the pier. Colin stood there and looked out over the lake.

Coronation Street wasn't one of Taffy's favourite programmes, but he had managed to sit through the first ten minutes of it. "This is crap. Does anyone fancy a game of cards or something?"

"Yeah, I'll play," said Numbnuts, who wasn't particularly bother about Coronation Street either.

"Norman?" asked Taffy.

Norman put down his copy of the TV times. "Yes, why not?"

"Lenny?"

Lenny had been deep in thought and only responded when his own name was mentioned. "Sorry, what did you say?"

"Do you fancy a game of cards?"

"Have you got any?"

"There will be some in the games room," suggested Norman.

The four men walked down the corridor to the games room. The fat man taking a pool shot didn't pay much attention to their arrival, but the short thin man with bleached blonde hair looked pleased to see them. He beamed a smile and waved a limp wrist.

"Who's that?" whispered Numbnuts.

"Oh no," said Taffy.

Lenny sniggered. "Is that...?"

"Fuck off," said Taffy. "Don't start."

A table was quickly found, and a pack of cards was brought from the cupboard in the corner.

"Right, what are we playing?" asked Norman as he shuffled the pack.

"Queeny," suggested Lenny with a smirk.

Taffy chose to ignore the remark.

"Ok then, what about..."

"What about solo?" interjected Numbnuts.

Everyone agreed and the cards were dealt.

"I'll pass," said Taffy.

"Me too."

"And me."

Norman considered his hand for a short while. "I'll pass as well."

The cards were returned to Lenny for another deal.

"What did he have to say then?" said Taffy casually as he picked up his cards.

"Who?"

"Charlie Marshall."

"I thought you said you didn't know Charlie Marshall," interrupted Norman.

"I don't. I was just having a game of chess with him, that's all."

"You want to keep away from him," suggested Norman.

"Why's that then?" asked Lenny, as he picked up his cards from the table and began arranging them into suits.

"I told you; he isn't very well liked. Nobody trusts him."

"I only talked to him because I was interested."

"Interested in what?" asked Taffy, adding, "what a load of crap" as he looked at his cards "I'll pass."

"Well, it's a bit strange, nicking a million quid and then turning yourself in. I'll go solo. I mean you've got to be thick or something."

"Charlie Marshall is far from thick," said Norman. "Think about it. How many people do you know who only get five years for armed robbery?"

"Yes, but what has he gained? He handed in his share of the money."

"Did he?" said Norman.

Lenny thought for a moment. "Well, yes. It was all in the papers. Charlie Marshall walked into a police station three days after the robbery with two hundred and fifty grand."

"Yes," said Norman, "but what happened to the rest?"

"The other two, his mates, they must've hidden it."

"If you think that you're as daft as the cops."

"Look," said Taffy, "are we gonna play cards or what?"

"I'll pass," said Numbnuts.

"Right Lenny, it's your lead."

The game went on for about twenty minutes without any mention of Charlie Marshall and would have gone on for longer, but for the intervention of a prison guard.

"Is one of you Leonard Grey?" said the guard.

"Yeah. That's me."

The guard checked the piece of paper he was holding. "5175, Grey. Right, come with me."

"What's up?" said Lenny as he rose to his feet.

"Nothing, Mr Wilson wants a word with you that's all."

Lenny followed the guard out of the door and down the corridor.

"Well," said Taffy, "that fucks that."

"It's alright," said a voice. "I'll take his place." Nick Green sat himself down in the seat that Lenny had vacated. "Right boys, what are we playing?"

As Nick beamed a smile, Taffy, Numbnuts and Norman looked at one another.

"I think I've had enough of cards," said Norman as he rose to his feet. "I think I'll go and watch some telly."

"Yes," said Taffy as he hurried after Norman, "there's that thing on."

"Yes, that's right," said Numbnuts stopping at the door to address Nick. "There's a thing on."

Nick Green sat alone with a puzzled look on his face. Eventually he raised his hands and sniffed his armpits.

Numbnuts on his way back from the prison library when the 8 o'clock bell rang and so he headed for his cell. To his surprise, Lenny was already there.

"Alright?" he said with his usual cheerful smile.

Lenny, who was laying on his bed reading, looked up from his book. "Alright?"

"What did Mr Wilson want?" asked Numbnuts as he perched himself on the edge of his bed.

"He er… He just wanted to let me know he's got me an appointment to see the governor in the morning."

"The governor? Why?"

"Probably nothing."

"It must be important if you're going to see the governor," Numbnuts persisted.

Lenny put his book down and propped himself up on one elbow. "Well, I don't want you saying anything, but there's a chance I may be let out for the day.!

Numbnuts looked positively excited at the news. "How come?"

"Well, it's a long story and I've been told not to get my hopes up."

A terrible thought crossed Numbnuts' mind: maybe there was something wrong at home, an illness or something. "Is everything alright?" he asked.

"Yes, everything's fine; I'll fill you in tomorrow."

Numbnuts was relieved everything was all right and decided to leave it at that.

"Hey look," he said holding up his two books, "I've been to the library."

"Really, what you got? Come here, let's have a look."

Lenny took the two books from Numbnuts and read the cover on the larger of the two. "*Guitar for the beginner!* You don't have a guitar."

"I know, but I've checked, and they do have guitar classes here. I'm going to join tomorrow."

Lenny handed *Guitar for the beginner* back to Numbnuts and read the title of the second book and laughed out loud. *Palmistry, the future revealed.*

"Yes. Wouldn't it be good to be able to see the future?"

"Let's have a go, shall we? Here, give us your hand," said Lenny. He took Numbnuts' hand and opened the book. "Hmm," he said as if concentrating hard. "I can see a green van… and wait… there's someone in the back." Lenny looked up at Numbnuts who was staring at his own hand. "It's you. The van is going up the hill to…the loony bin."

Numbnuts snatched the book away and lay back on the bed. "I take it you don't believe in fortune telling," he said grumpily.

"Course not. It's all a load of codswallop."

"That's where you're wrong. I used to know a very good fortune-teller called Madam Moat. She was a friend of mi mother."

"Do I know her? What's her first name?"

"Betty."

"Betty Moet," said Lenny mockingly.

"Yes, she used to live in Rotherham near mi mother. I used to see her when I visited mi mam."

"And?"

"And what?"

"Was she any good?"

Numbnuts thought carefully. "I don't know. I suppose she did get a few things wrong." He paused for a moment before continuing, "she predicted me, and our Sandra would have kids." Numbnuts paused again. "Two boys she said, both with bright red hair, like mine, at least like mine used to be."

Lenny sensed sadness in his friend's voice. "You know, Danny, having kids isn't always what it's cracked up to be. Changing nappies, sitting up worrying about them… you have to rearrange your whole life around them."

"Yeah, I know… sounds great."

"She may have been right though," added Lenny deciding to change tactics. "There's plenty of time for you and your Sandra to have kids."

Numbnuts half-heartedly nodded his agreement. "Yeah, I suppose."

"I hope she was wrong about the hair though," said Lenny with a smile.

"Yeah, poor little buggers."

"Anyway, tell me more about the Madam Moet. What else did she predict? Did she get anything right?"

"Well, the last time I spoke to her she did say I would never see her alive again. I suppose that was true."

"What, she predicted her own death?"

"Not exactly, she moved to Blackpool to open her own shop."

Numbnuts saw the look of utter bewilderment on Lenny's face and decided to explain in a little more detail. "I know what you're thinking, and I thought the same; anyone could have predicted that if they knew they were moving away. So, a couple of years ago I decided to go to Blackpool and visit Madam Moat's shop, you know, to tempt fate I suppose. I figured if I got to see her, her prediction would be proved wrong. But I never did."

"So, she did die."

"I don't know really. When I got to her shop, it was closed."

"Didn't you go back later or anything?"

"No point really; there was a sign on the door saying, 'Closed due to unforeseen circumstances'."

Lenny puzzled for a moment until he saw a grin on Numbnuts' face.

"Fuck off." Lenny lay back on his bed and lifted his book as a thought crossed his mind. Lenny dismissed it. Of course, Numbnuts was kidding, wasn't he?

An owl hooted out its joy at catching a small shrew on the far bank of the boating lake, but Colin didn't hear it. He had hit the water with a loud splash. The ice-cold water that filled his ears now filled his mouth and his nostrils as he lay in the thick mud at the bottom of the lake. The splash he had made caught the interest of the owl, which scanned the area around the old pier with her night vision. She saw nothing untoward, just a few ripples on the surface of the water working their way out to the middle of the lake. The ripples died away. Everything was calm and quiet, and the owl turned her attention back to the shrew. She had only taken one bite out of her catch when another noise startled her, forcing her to turn her attention back to the old pier. Something had erupted from the water with a loud gasp. The something rose to its feet; water cascaded down its body on its return to the lake. The owl decided there were better places to eat a shrew, and prey in tow, flew off towards the graveyard.

Colin, who by now had managed to stand upright, looked down at the lake. Although, its circumference was almost a mile and a half, its depth was, apparently, only two feet!

As he stood there trying to make sense of what had just happened, his bottom lip began to quiver.

The boating lake was man made thought Colin. They had probably only dug it this shallow for fear of children falling overboard.

Colin was unsure what to do next; his teeth began to chatter. He knew he wouldn't be able to drown himself in two feet of water. He looked at the large rock he was still holding to his chest; he would no longer be needing that, and anyway, it was getting heavy.

Colin released the rock. It splashed into the lake sending a plume of water up into his face. Almost immediately, Colin felt pain as the rock broke two of his toes on his good foot.

Chapter Seven

Swag

It was 8am and the prison bell rang out, its wake-up call, a call that Lenny and Numbnuts did not need; they had been awake since dawn. Today was Saturday, and Saturday was visiting day. Lenny and Numbnuts sat on the edge of their beds eagerly waiting for their cell door to be unlocked. Nothing much was said because, although they didn't want to admit it, both were very nervous at the prospect of a visit from their wives. Numbnuts wondered if Sandra was going to come at all. This doubt had begun to grow in his mind after his last telephone call with her. She had been so upset that she told him she never wanted to see him again. At the time, Numbnuts had dismissed this, but as time went on, he was beginning to wonder if she had really meant it. Lenny was wondering if there would be enough prison guards present to stop Sue from Killing him. At 8:09am they heard the turning of a key in the cell door and a prison officer entered.

"5175 Grey," said Lenny, who was by now getting used to the routine.

"5176 Harrison," said Numbnuts. The guard ticked off their names and headed to the next cell, leaving the door open.

"Shall we have breakfast?" asked Lenny. The dining room was full. It seemed everyone wanted to get breakfast early that morning and Taffy was no exception. He was already seated when Lenny and Numbnuts arrived, and signalled his presence by waving across the dining room. Lenny joined the queue at the serving area and Numbnuts followed.

"Good morning," said the man in front.

Lenny responded before looking up. "Good morning...oh it's you."

"Who did you except?" asked Charlie. "Lord Lucan?"

Lenny didn't answer.

"I enjoyed our little game yesterday; perhaps we could play again sometime."

Lenny thought about Norman's warning to keep away from Charlie Marshall. "I don't know," he said. "I'm not in here for long and I don't know if it would be a good idea to..."

"Ah," said Charlie looking at Norman who had just joined the end of the queue, "I see, people have been talking."

"It's just that..."

"It's just that," interrupted Charlie, "you've been warned off associating with me. Interesting. I thought you were the kind to choose his own company." Charlie spooned a ladle full of beans on to his plate and left for the dining area.

Charie's departing comment had struck a chord with Lenny who was now deep in thought and inadvertently holding up the queue.

"Are you having any breakfast or not?" asked Numbnuts impatiently.

Lenny filled his plate with bacon, egg and sausage and went off in the same direction as Charlie.

"You're right I do pick up my own company," said Lenny as he sat himself down next to Charlie Marshall.

Charlie smiled and went about his breakfast. After a few minutes, Charlie washed his breakfast down with a mouthful of tea and spoke. "So how is Malton?"

"Much the same, I suppose," said Lenny. "Just as boring as ever."

"Nice place to go in the summer was Malton, picnics up by the boating lake."

"I suppose you know it well then, do you?"

"Oh yes. I used to work for the Parish Council. I planted all the flowerbeds on the west embankment. Did they turn out all right?"

"Yes, they looked really nice. Haven't you seen them?"

"No. I was in here before they flowered."

"Oh."

"Father O'Connor, is he still the priest?"

"Yes, but I don't see that much of him. I don't go to church much," confessed Lenny.

"Me neither."

"So, what exactly did you do for the council?" asked Lenny as he took a sip of his own tea.

"A bit of all sorts really, gardening mainly. You work for the colliery, don't you?"

"Yeah." Lenny thought for a moment. "Well, sort of. We're on strike at the moment."

"Yes, I've been watching it on the news. Tragic."

"Yes. Anyone visiting you today?" asked Lenny in an attempt to change the subject away from the strike, a subject that always depressed him.

"No, I don't get many visitors these days."

"You not married then?" asked Lenny.

"No. My…err, my wife died three years ago." Lenny detected a hint of sadness in Charlie's voice and for the first time since Lenny had met him, he appeared vulnerable and unsure of himself.

"I'm sorry."

"Cancer," Charlie went on. "Quite sudden. Elizabeth was only forty-nine."

"Kids?" asked Lenny in the hope that the thought of his children would cheer him up a little.

"A son, David"

"Doesn't he visit?"

"No. I think he feels I let him down a bit, you know, getting sent to prison and that. He lives with his uncle now. You having any visitors today?"

"Yeah, my wife's coming."

"You got kids?"

"A girl, Lisa. She's five."

"Does she know you're in here?"

"No." Lenny thought for a moment and looked slightly worried. "At least, I don't think so."

"Good," said Charlie. "Keep it that way."

"So," said Lenny, deciding to change the subject again, "how much longer are you in for?"

"Well, I'm eligible for parole next year. Not that many get it for the first time round, but still, it's a possibility."

"We get out Christmas Eve."

“Yes, I’ve heard. Quite a few going out in the next couple of weeks. I expect most of them to be back in though.” Charlie pointed best he could with his teacup. “Him for example, he’s a definite.”

Lenny looked in the direction of Charlie’s teacup and observed a tall thin man with white hair. Lenny recognised the man as Charlie’s chess opponent. The man, who was well into his sixties, was pouring himself a cup of tea from the stainless steal urn in the corner.

“Why? Asked Lenny. “Is he a gangster or something?”

“Not really, he’s just greedy, no patience.”

“What do you mean? Who is he?”

“That’s Peter Bellis; he’s in for fraud and deception. He had quite a good scam going back in the seventies, selling cut price exclusive holidays to the rich and wealthy.”

“What’s wrong with that?”

“The holidays didn’t exist. Peter hired a shop then went round collecting holiday brochures from legitimate travel agents and filled his own shop with them. Then he started taking bookings for Caribbean holidays that he didn’t have, simple really.”

“What happened? How did he get caught?”

“Greed. He was making a fortune, but he went on too long. He was still taking bookings when he had holidays beginning to fall through, a matter of time really.”

“And you reckon he’ll be back inside?”

“Peter Bellis goes out next Wednesday.” Charlie thought for a moment. “He’ll be lucky if he’s not back inside by the New Year.”

“What makes you so sure?”

“Because he’s greedy. If he hadn’t been so greedy, he wouldn’t have been caught in the first place. And I happen to know that the police didn’t recover all of the money. Twenty grand not accounted for I heard, and if I know that, the police know that.”

Lenny looked a little confused. “So what?”

“So, they will be watching him when he gets out. Peter knows that, but being a greedy and impatient man, he won’t be able to keep away from it. He will lead them straight to it. He’ll be caught in possession of stolen money whilst on licence from prison and he'll be back for the New Year!"

"And what about you? Will you be back?"

Charlie smiled. "Look at me, I'm nearly sixty; I can't afford another stretch inside. No, I've retired. I was thinking of emigrating, somewhere warm, perhaps making amends with my son, and the rest of my family."

Lenny rose to his feet. He was glad he decided to sit with Charlie. The truth was he hadn't liked Charlie much after their first encounter, but today for some reason, Charlie seemed a little less sure of himself, a little less arrogant.

"I've got to go," said Lenny. "Visiting time in half an hour. Perhaps we could have a game later."

Charlie looked up and smiled. "I'd like that."

Lenny, Numbnuts and Taffy sat on the benches that lined the long corridor outside the visitor's hall, along with twenty other prisoners. The clock on the wall at the end of the corridor ticked slowly towards ten o'clock. Lenny and Numbnuts sat quietly contemplating their fate. Taffy who had removed a shoe was trying to smell his foot.

"What are you doing?" asked Lenny.

Taffy pushed his foot towards his friend. "Do my feet smell?"

Lenny backed away. "I don't want to smell your feet."

Taffy tried once more to smell his foot before putting it back into its shoe.

Lenny looked up at the clock. "Two minutes," he said to Numbnuts, who has been quietest of all. Numbnuts nodded in acknowledgment.

"Taffy, what the fuck is wrong with you?"

Taffy, who was sitting with both hands in the air, was now trying to sniff his own armpits. "Do I smell?"

"Yes," said Lenny immediately, "but you always do."

"I'll have to get a shower."

"Haven't you had one yet? We've been in here five days."

"No." Taffy thought for a while. "Shall we all go for a shower this afternoon?"

"I've had a shower."

"What, on your own?"

"Yes. Why, what's the problem?"

"You shouldn't go for a shower on your own, not in here."

"Why?"

"Things can happen to people in prison showers, especially if you're pretty."

"Well, you should be alright then."

The minute the hand clicked on to one minute as Lenny looked at Numbnuts. "You alright?"

Numbnuts nodded his head. "We had a fight you know, on the telephone. She was crying. I don't even know if she's going to come."

Lenny placed his hand on his friend's shoulder. "Course she going to come."

"Does my hair look alright?" asked Taffy.

Lenny and Numbnuts answered in unison, "NO."

"Who's visiting you anyway?" asked Lenny.

"Angie," Taffy replied with the grin of a particularly pleased Cheshire cat.

"What, from behind the bar?"

"Yeah."

Lenny shook his head. "Wonders never cease."

The clock clicked on to ten o'clock and the doors at the end of the corridor opened.

The inmates followed the six prison officers who had been waiting at the end of the corridor into a large assembly room. The room was quite spacious with large windows overlooking the sports field at the back of the prison. Dotted around the room were tables and chairs where friends and families of the inmates were quietly waiting. Lenny looked around and was pleased to see Numbnuts' Sandra at one of the tables by the window. Sandra waved then pointed across the room to the table where Sue was waiting.

Lenny pointed out Sandra to Numbnuts then set off towards his own wife. He sat down across the table from Sue and smiled. "Hello." Then, quite unexpectedly, a wave of guilt overcame him. Lenny didn't understand why. Maybe it was something inside of him, something he had been suppressing for days, but the sight of

Sue sitting opposite him had allowed it out. Lenny felt so ashamed; he didn't understand that either. He knew what he had done wasn't so bad, but he couldn't stop his eyes filling with tears.

"I'm so sorry," he said as he lowered his head.

Sue reached across the table, squeezed his hand and smiled. "You silly beggar."

Sue's visit had gone well. She had brought with her a picture of Lenny standing by a large crane with the words *My Dad by Lisa Grey* untidily written across the top of the paper. Sue had explained that the crane was because Lisa was under the impression that her father had gone to work away for a short while (a little white lie that Lenny was grateful for). Lenny had assured Sue that prison wasn't as bad as he had expected and she in return had assured him that she was all right. They had talked about their daughter, how Sandra was coping, and about the vicious rumour that had apparently been started by Liz Fisher about Taffy burgling a couple of pensioners. "Needless to say," said Sue, "no one believes it."

By the time the clock reached twelve and it was time to say their goodbyes, Lenny was left wondering where the morning had gone, although he hadn't much time to dwell on it due to his 12:30 appointment with the governor.

"I've told you," said Mr Wilson as they walked along the top corridor to the governor's office, "it's a very unusual request."

"But he might allow it," said Lenny hopefully. "Has he got kids?"

"As a matter of fact, he has, but I can't see that influencing his decision."

Eventually they reached the reception desk at the end of the hall. The young lady behind the desk, who Lenny presumed to be the governor's secretary, smiled up at them.

"5175 Grey," said Mr Wilson as he handed the secretary some paperwork.

"The governors expecting you, Mr Wilson," she said.

"Thank you, Mary." Mr Wilson turned to Lenny, "Now wait here."

Lenny watched as Mr Wilson walked past the two prison guards seated behind the reception desk, knock on, and then disappear through a large oak door at the end of the corridor.

"What's he like?" asked Lenny.

"Who?" answered the secretary as she loaded some paper into the photocopier.

"The governor."

"He's really nice, considering."

Lenny didn't like the considering bit. "Considering what?"

"Well," said the secretary, "it's not my place to say really."

Lenny was just wondering whether to press the issue when Mr Wilson reappeared.

"This was Grey."

The two prison guards rose to their feet and accompanied Lenny into the governors' office.

Mr Wilson closed the door behind them and took a seat in the corner. The prison guards took up position on both sides and slightly forward of Lenny. Lenny waited for the governor, who was seated behind a large Edwardian-style desk, to finish whatever it was that he was reading.

The décor of the governor's spacious office matched his desk. The walls were lined with wooden panels on which hung a number of oil portraits of what Lenny assumed to be, previous governors of the prison. Lenny reached this conclusion after noticing that the portrait at the end was of the man who now sat before him quietly studying some papers. Lenny waited some more. Eventually the governor put down the papers, sat back into his excessively large leather chair and stared up at Lenny.

"I must say, Grey, this is a most unusual request."

"They are the most unusual circumstances," replied Lenny hopefully.

The governor thought for a while before answering. "Granted, but I am not given to granting home visits merely on unusual circumstances. I'm afraid home visits can only be authorised if I believe it to be of psychological benefit to the offender or the offender's family."

"I understand that."

"Well," said the governor as he briefly reviewed the papers. "I don't see anything here that falls within those criteria."

Lenny almost expected the words, "Request denied" to follow, but they didn't. Instead, the governor remained silent, as if willing Lenny to find a loophole in the rulebook.

Lenny took great encouragement from this and thought hard. "Well," he said as an idea began to form in his head, "my daughter attends that school."

Lenny awaited a response, but none was forthcoming.

"And," he continued, as he waited for the idea to take shape, "I would say, that it would have a great psychological impact on her if the school Christmas party was cancelled due to her father's imprisonment."

The governor raised his eyebrows as he considered Lenny's argument. "But would the party be cancelled due to your absence?" he asked.

Lenny was about to assure the governor that it would when Mr Wilson politely coughed and rose to his feet. "I have been advised by the headmistress, a Mrs Taylor, that with such short notice the event would be cancelled." Mr Wilson returned to his seat and the governor to his notes.

"You put me in an awkward predicament Grey. The truth of the matter is that I just don't have the manpower at the moment."

Lenny could feel things taking a turn for the worse. "Come on," he couldn't help saying, "these kids have got nowt!" Lenny found the step he had taken close to the governor deliberately blocked by the two guards. Lenny took a deep breath and recomposed himself. "Look, these kids, all their families work at the pit. They've had nothing all year, and whether you agree with the strike or not, it's not their fault. We just wanted them to have one good day, that's all, just one good day in a year. They've had to give up so much."

The governor sat quietly for a long time before removing his pencil from his mouth. "I'm sorry; I just haven't got the manpower." Lenny's heart sank. "Unless," added the governor, " I were able to get a couple of officers from my staff who would be prepared to accompany you on their day off."

Lenny realised that the governor was no longer looking at him. Instead, his eyes were shifting back and forth between the two prison officers. The two officers look at each other before one of them spoke.

"What day would it be, Sir?"

"Wednesday the 20th I believe." The governor checked his notes. "Yes, the 20th."

"That's my day off, Sir. I would be happy to accompany Mr Grey." The officer looked at his comrade.

Eventually the other officer responded, all be it a little less enthusiastically. "Me too, Sir."

"Very well," said the governor, signing the bottom of an official looking document, which he then held out for Mr Wilson to retrieve, "request granted. I'll leave it with Mr Wilson to make the final preparations."

The two officers turned to face the door and indicated to Lenny to do the same. Lenny moved towards the door then stopped and turn back towards the governor. There was something he'd forgotten to say. "Merry Christmas, Governor."

The governor sat back in his chair and smiled. "Merry Christmas to you, Mr Grey."

Numbnuts entered his cell to find Lenny blu-tacking his daughter's picture to the wall.

"I've done it," said Lenny, clenching his fist in front of himself, "I've only gone and bloody don't it!"

Lenny was so happy that Numbnuts felt a smile being forced across his own face.

"Done what?"

"I'm going home on Wednesday."

"Great," said Numbnuts who was beginning to get caught up in Lenny's enthusiasm. Enthusiasm faded to satisfaction and satisfaction found itself being replaced by worry over the course of a few seconds as Numbnuts began to wonder why his friend thought he might be going home. "Why's that then?" He slowly asked as worry crumbled to fear. "You're not thinking of escaping, are you? We've only got eight days left. Come on, we can do it it's not so..."

"I'm not going to escape. I've been granted a home visit."

Numbnuts looked suspicious. “A what?”

“A home visit. I told you the other day, they’re letting me out for the day.”

“Why?”

“Because of the kids.”

“What fuckin’ kids?”

“The kids at our Lisa’s school.”

“What about them?”

“I’m being let out to see them.”

“Why?”

“Because I’m Father Christmas.”

Numbnuts stood in stunned silence. Eventually he took Lenny by the arm. “Do you want to sit down for a bit?”

Lenny shook his arm free. “Look, it’s the kids’ Christmas party the day after tomorrow and I’m supposed to be playing Santa for them. So, they’re letting me out for the day on compassionate grounds.”

“That’s brilliant! When did you think of that?”

“I didn’t, it’s true.”

“What, you playing Santa! Since when?”

“I agreed to do it last week.”

Numbnuts sat on the bed and shook his head in amazement. “I don’t believe it.”

Lenny went back to sticking the picture on the wall.

“Hey, perhaps they’ll let me, and Taffy go as a couple of reindeer… what do you think?”

Lenny spent the rest of the day, and the day after that with a huge smile on his face. He was still grinning on the morning of the children’s party.

“Bastard,” said Taffy as he miscued, leaving a relatively easy black, which Lenny went on to pot.

“It’s not your day, is it Taff? Set ‘em up.”

“You set ‘em up,” protested Taffy. “I set ‘em up last time.”

“That’s because you lost last time.”

“So?”

“So, loser sets ‘em up.”

Taffy begrudgingly took the balls from beneath the pool table and began to arrange them in their triangle. "Where's Numbnuts?" he inquired.

"He's having a guitar lesson."

"Still on with that crap, is he?"

"Yep." Lenny chalked his cue. "It's your break."

"I've been thinking of going to one of them classes," declared Taffy as he sent the cue ball crashing into the pack.

"What? Music classes?"

"No, computers."

"What do you want to know about computers for?"

"Because that's where the future is. I've been talking to people."

"What people?"

"Terry Wild for a start."

Lenny got the impression he should know who Terry Wild was.

"And," continued Taffy, "he said there was a lot of money to be made from computers."

"Who the fuck is Terry Wild?"

"Oh, he's a friend of Arsenic."

"And what does he know about computers?"

"Well, he was caught with a van full."

"And that makes him an expert, does it?"

"No...but he's right in what he says, computers are the future."

"Why?"

"Computer fraud is a growing industry, ask anyone in here.

Lenny shook his head. "So, you want to get into computers so you can embezzle money?"

"Yeah. Why else would people in here bother with a computer course? Come to think of it it's pretty funny really."

"What is?"

"Coming in here and doing classes. All the ex-car thieves have joined the mechanics class to find out how to hot wire different makes of car, and all your burglars are doing electronics to learn how to overcome alarm systems."

Lenny pondered for a moment before taking his shot. “You’re so fuckin’ cynical,” he said as he once more potted the black to win another game.

Lenny looked at his watch, 10 o’clock; three hours to go, he thought.

“I’m fed up with this, let’s go and see what’s on telly,” suggested Taffy.

Lenny and Taffy found the TV room empty except for the solitary figure of Charlie Marshall who was sitting at the back table with his chessboard at the ready.

“Waiting for someone?” asked Lenny.

“Yes,” said Charlie as he looked down at his watch. “I’ve arranged to give Peter a game before he leaves.”

Taffy made his way over to the TV and turned it on, but Lenny decided to stay and talk to Charlie for a moment.

“Peter who?” he asked.

“Peter Bellis. He hasn’t beaten me for three years and today’s his last chance.”

Lenny pulled up a chair. “That’s right, that’s the guy you were telling me about. He’s getting out today, is he?”

“Yeah. Tell me Lenny, do you think I should let him win?”

Lenny thought for a moment. “Nah, what’s the point?”

“Well, I have shared a cell with him for two years; it could be a sort of going away present.”

Charlie’s decision on whether or not to throw the game was interrupted by one of the prison officers who entered the room carrying a bunch of letters.

“Charlie,” said the officer handing Charlie a letter before leaving.

Charlie thanked the officer and opened the letter. Lenny sat quietly as Charlie read through it and was surprised to witness a look of great disappointment appear on Charlie’s face.

“Not bad news I hope,” said Lenny, but Charlie didn’t seem to hear him. Lenny watched as Charlie’s eyes began to well up. Charlie’s look of shock and depression changed to a look of embarrassment as he pulled himself back from wherever it was he had been.

"You'll have to excuse me," Charlie rose to his feet and headed for the door.

Lenny noticed that Charlie had left behind his chess set and the letter. He called after him, but it was too late, Charlie had gone.

Lenny resisted the temptation to read the letter. Instead, he opted to put it back into its envelope and return it later. However, as he pushed the letter back into its envelope, he couldn't help but noticing the stamp. It wasn't the usual queen's head stamp that he was used to; it was bright orange and a lot bigger, and the picture on it appeared to be of a broken eggshell. He put the letter in his pocket, packed up the chess set and joined Taffy in front of the TV.

'Why do I always get the one with the chuffin' wonky wheel?' Janet asked herself as she struggled with a supermarket trolley that seemed to have developed a mind of its own. "Sodding thing," she muttered as she took a pit stop by the frozen foods. She was in the middle of deciding whether or not to go back and get a new trolley when she noticed Numbnuts' Sandra by the fruit and veg. Janet was about to wave a greeting in order to catch Sandra's attention when she realised that Sandra was not alone.

A tall man with a Mediterranean look about him had engaged Sandra in conversation. Janet recognised the man immediately; it was Georgio, the milkman. Feeling it would be rude to interrupt their conversation, she decided to spy on them for a little while instead. Janet slipped behind one of the up-standing refrigerators.

Georgio was smiling like Janet had never seen him smile before, his teeth looking unnaturally white against his dark complexion. Janet watched as Georgio picked up one of the cucumbers from the rack and waved it suggestively in front of himself. Janet was quite taken back by Georgio's behaviour; she had always known him as a quiet man who didn't seem to mix with people. Georgio placed the cucumber into Sandra's trolley and, leaning over as if not to be overheard, said something that sent Sandra into hysterical laughter. Janet had seen enough. She had something to give Sandra: a piece of her mind. Janet grabbed her trolley and headed straight for Sandra, but her trolley headed straight for the baked beans.

The clattering of cans caught everyone's attention, including Sandra and Georgio's. they hurried over to help pick up the cans.

"What you doing?" asked Sandra picking up a stray can that Janet had missed.

"What am *I* doing?" said Janet sternly. "What the bloody hell are *you* doing?"

Sandra looked puzzled. "Shopping!"

Janet snatched the cucumber from Sandra's trolley as if it were a smoking gun.

"What's this then?"

"It's a cucumber."

"Yes but," said Janet, who knew what she meant, but at the same time didn't, "what's it all about?"

Sandra looked a little confused. "It's for making salads."

"Oh yeah and what's so funny about that then?" Janet question was directed at Georgio.

"Are you alright?" asked Sandra.

"Come on, what's so funny about cucumbers?"

Georgio looked at Sandra as if to confirm that it was all right to answer. "Nothing," he said innocently. "I just said I've got one bigger than that."

"I knew it! Poor old Numbnuts is locked up and you take the opportunity to impress his wife with the size of your manhood. Well, I'll tell you something mister, it takes a dammed sight more than a week without a man, before a woman is willing to drop her knickers for the likes of you!" There were a few seconds of awkward silence before Janet added, "You ought to be ashamed of yourselves!"

Georgio reached into the basket and produced a large cucumber; he held it alongside the one in Janet's hand for comparison. "I mean I've got one bigger."

Georgio put his cucumber away, bid Janet and Sandra good day and headed for the fresh meat counter.

"Well," said Sandra, "I hope you're proud of yourself. He was only having a laugh."

"I was just trying to look out for you," said Janet timidly. "I thought you might be getting a bit, you know, frustrated, and I didn't want him taking advantage..."

"Seems to me you're the one who's getting frustrated. I'll see you later."

Sandra walked away leaving Janet feeling awkward and in the possession of an under-ripe cucumber.

"You've forgotten your cucumber," Janet called after her.

Sandra's reply came without her even bothering to turn around. "Keep it, Janet; I think you need it more than me!"

Janet was left alone and embarrassed. Maybe Sandra was right. Maybe there wasn't anything going on; maybe it was just a bit of innocent fun; maybe it was her own sexual frustration that had made her overreact. Janet walked over to the fruit and veg stand, intending to replace the cucumber in its rack. 'Never liked the bloody things anyway,' she said to herself, looking at the offending vegetable. 'They give me chuffin' hiccups.' Suddenly she stopped as if to consider something. Then, after looking around, Janet quickly placed a cucumber in her trolley and set off towards the checkout.

Lenny unwrapped the brown paper parcel that Sue had given him during her visit and took out the crimson suit. He put it on and after adjusting the wires that attached the long white beard to his ears, stood in front of the full-length mirrors that were situated on the far wall of the gymnasium changing room.

Taffy and Numbnuts applauded and giggled.

"I feel a right pillock," said Lenny.

"You look a right pillock," agreed Taffy.

The door to the changing room swung open and two prison guards entered. "Here, we've brought you this," said Mr Turner with a proud smile.

"It's a sack," added Mr Phillips.

Lenny took the sack and held it aloft. "Thanks, what is it?"

"A sack," repeated Mr Phillips. "You know, what Santa has."

"Thanks," said Lenny unappreciatively, "but I think the school has a proper one, you know, with presents in."

"We know; it's just something for you to carry as you arrive."

Lenny held the sack aloft again and looked at it. "But it's empty."

"Ah," said Mr Turner, his proud smile deserting him. After a few seconds, his smile returned, and he searched through a bunch of keys that hung from his belt. "I've got an idea, wait here."

Mr Turner unlocked the door to the laundry room and disappeared inside, reappearing moments later with his arms full of muddy football shirts.

"Open it up then!" he commanded.

Lenny held open the sack and the shirts were bundled inside; Lenny slung the sack over his shoulder and looked in the mirror once again.

"That's better," said Mr Turner.

Suddenly, Taffy rushed over and started to pick up the unwanted shirts from the floor. "Here, put these on."

"What?"

"Go on. You're too thin, they'll make you fatter."

"I'm not putting them on, they're dirty."

"They'll be under your suit," protested Taffy as he pushed several shirts into Lenny's arms.

"No way."

"Fine, well just tell the kids Santa's anorexic!"

A few minutes later, Lenny was standing in front of the mirror looking decidedly fatter. Although it was hard to move, he had to agree it was a good idea.

Lenny was ready to go. Mr Turner and Mr Phillips were waiting by the door.

"Good luck then," said Numbnuts with a smile.

"Yeah." Lenny checked himself one last time.

"Say hello to everyone for us," said Taffy as he sat tossing a stick of chalk, which he'd picked up from the chalkboard at the end of the changing room, into the air.

"If I can." Lenny slung the sack over his shoulder and walked through the changing room doors.

Taffy and Numbnuts roared with laughter as the doors swung shut.

Mr Turner and Mr Phillips accompanied Lenny down various corridors. To Lenny's bewilderment, every prisoner they passed burst out laughing. He wondered what was so funny. Eventually, they went through the final gate that led to reception. Mr Turner and Mr Phillips stood at the swinging doors that lead to the courtyard. Lenny turned to see that the guard who was locking the gate through which he had just passed, was doubled up with laughter.

'What's everyone laughing at?' Lenny asked himself.

While Lenny was still wondering, Mr Turner took his arm and clicked shut one side of a pair of handcuffs around his wrist. As he closed the other end around his own wrist, Mr Turner noticed the surprised look on Lenny's face.

"Prison rules I'm afraid, don't take it personally. Any time we are outdoors we have to do this," he explained.

Lenny and his two guards passed through the glass doors, into the car park and made their way over to one of the blue prison vans that were parked behind steel gates in a secure section of the car park.

Mr Turner unlocked the handcuffs and opened the back doors of the van.

"Hello," said a man who was patiently waiting outside.

Lenny nodded at the man who was dressed in a velvet jacket with overly wide lapels.

"This is Peter Bellis," explained Mr Turner, unfastening Lenny's handcuffs. "He's being released; we're giving him a lift."

Lenny climbed into the van and Mr Turner locked the door behind him before joining his colleague in the front.

Peter puzzled over Lenny's costume for a short while before he spoke. "Are they... are they letting you out today?"

"Yes," replied Lenny in a matter of fact manner. "They let me out every Christmas you know, to deliver presents!"

"Oh," said Peter, with a nervous smile.

Lenny heard the engine of the van start up and felt a slight judder as it pulled away.

"Yes, we're just off to pick up the reindeer and then we're off delivering."

"Nice."

Lenny shook his head. "I'm having you on." Lenny held out his hand, "I'm Lenny."

Peter took Lenny's hand and gave a sigh of relief. "I'm Peter. Peter Bellis,"

"Yeah, I know; you're Charlie Marshall's cellmate."

"*Was* Charlie's cellmate," Peter corrected.

"Charlies told me all about you."

"Nothing bad I hope."

"No, not really, just that you were getting out today."

Peter was looking hard into Lenny's face. "Excuse me, have we met?"

Lenny removed his beard, which didn't seem to help; Peter stared even harder. "No, we haven't met; I've only been in a few days."

"Are you one of the men from Brookly?" inquired Peter.

"Well, Malton. Brookly's just down the road."

"Ah yes, Charlie has spoken of you. Tell me, have you seen anything of Charlie today? I was supposed to meet him for a game of chess, but I must have missed him."

"He was in the TV room earlier, but he..." Lenny wondered whether to mention the letter but decided against it, "he had to go."

"It's a pity; I was quite looking forward to our last game."

Peter was feeling more at ease now that he had decided that Lenny wasn't mad. "Excuse me but why are you dressed like that?"

"I could ask you the same question!" Lenny was looking at Peter's kipper tie.

"Yes," said Peter looking down at himself. "I suppose I do look a little dated, don't I. This is what I was wearing when I was locked up. I suppose fashions have altered."

"Just a bit," said Lenny sarcastically. Turning his attention back to his own attire he explained, "I'm going to a school. It's for the kids, sort of a compassionate leave."

"I see."

"Yes, it's my daughter's school."

"So, you'll get to see your daughter. That will be nice."

"And you?" asked Lenny. "Where are you bound for?"

"I'm going to stay with my sister for a while. I need to raise a little capital for a business venture."

"I thought you had a little capital," interrupted Lenny. "You know, stashed away."

Peter looked shocked and uncomfortable. He turned to the partition at the front of the cab and wondered how thin it was. "Who told you that?" he snapped in a whispered voice.

"It was just something Charlie mentioned."

"Charlie! Charlie told you that? Charlie has some need to talk." Peter sounded very angry.

"What do you mean Charlie has some need to talk?"

"Well, you would think that someone who wanted his own affairs kept private would respect the privacy of others, that's all."

"Are you talking about the missing million? Has he got it?"

"Of course he's got it," said Peter whose mind now seemed elsewhere, probably wondering who else Charlie had been talking to.

"Has he told you he's got it?"

"What! No, of course not! You don't admit to having that kind of money, not in prison. There are too many nasty people who will go to any lengths... if they couldn't intimidate Charlie, they could have someone on the outside get at his family. Has he said anything else about me?"

"No not really.... Then how do you know he's got it?"

Peter smiled. "I have been a con man all my life, and I know a con when I see it."

"What do you mean a con?"

"Charlie has conned everyone. The gang members, the police, even the courts. Charlie Marshall had no intention of taking that money and going on the run. He was quite prepared to take a light sentence and live the rest of his life as a millionaire, a FREE millionaire."

"But," said Lenny as he tried to remember what Charlie had told him, "Charlie didn't even know they'd nicked a million. They never even counted it; he heard the details on the radio." Lenny thought a little more. "He handed his share in as soon as he found out."

"Really," said Peter knowingly, "and how do you hand in your share of money that you haven't even counted?"

"What do you mean?"

"I mean, if you don't know how much you've stolen, how can you have a share in the first place?"

Lenny could see the logic, but he was still a little confused. "What about the rest of the gang?"

"What about them? They're doing thirty years in Wormwood Scrubs; Charlie made sure of that at the trial. He told the jury that the guns they were carrying were loaded. He said he'd refused to carry one and had made an excuse to the gang that if he was to be the driver a gun would get in his way. He said he had made this excuse because he was in fear of his own life. The thing is, Charlie didn't do the driving. Charlie can't drive. Charlie will have twenty-five years and a million pounds head start on the rest of the gang!"

Peter contemplated that for a moment. "Perhaps that's why he was always talking about emigrating."

Lenny sat quietly and asked himself if he would be prepared to spend five years in prison for a million pounds. He had to conclude that he would not, but then again, he wasn't Charlie Marshall.

Lenny felt the van slow down and eventually stop.

"The funny thing is..." said Peter rubbing his chin.

"What?"

"Well, it's his family."

"What about his family?" asked Lenny.

Peter was just about to speak when the doors of the van were thrown open and the smiling face of Mr Turner peered in at them. "Here we are Peter."

Peter shook Lenny's hand and climbed from the van.

"See you soon," said Lenny with a grin.

"Hope not," replied Peter giving his velvet jacket a quick brush down. The doors of the van were closed, and Lenny was left alone to wonder a little more about Charlie Marshall.

Dear Father Christmas

Me and my brother have been good my mum says. And so, I would like a Leeds United football shirt and sum boots. I know that my dad and mum haven't got any money this year bicouse of Margerat Thatcher but my dad says we are better of than most bicouse he is the bos of the union and oure garage is full of food and if you come to my house I will leave you a mince pie. My name is John Beach and I live at 26 Lime Grove.

John Beach's letter to Santa, which had been posted on the classroom wall, along with a great number of similar letters, was causing a great deal of controversy.

"What does he mean his dads got a garage full of food? Who's his dad?" asked one irate woman.

"John Beach... that'll be Mick Beach's lad," answered another.

"How come he's got a garage full of food?"

"It could be for the food parcels," suggested a third.

"Food parcels my arse. Might be what he's held back; might be stuff we should have had."

"I know Mick Beach, he wouldn't do that," protested one of the men,

The classroom door opened and Mrs Taylor the headmistress appeared. "Mums, dads, boys and girls," she said beaming a nervous smile at everyone, "Santa is about to arrive."

Everyone left the classroom and walked down the corridor that led to the main doors. Mrs Taylor popped into several classrooms along the way to pass on the word to other parents and children.

Eventually everyone was gathered outside the school, patiently awaiting Santa's arrival.

"Someone should have a word with that Mick Beach," whispered one of the women to her husband.

"They're just kids, who knows what they're thinking. Mick might keep his freezer in the garage for all we know."

Mrs Taylor looked at her watch.

Sue and Janet, who were standing on the fringes of the crowd, looked at each other. "You don't think he's bottled it do you?" asked Janet.

"Course not; he was looking forward to it."

"I'm cold mummy," protested Lisa as she snuggled up to her mother's leg.

"I know darling, but Santa will be here any minute now, we don't want to miss him do we?"

Lisa shook her head and Sue gave her a cuddle.

At the back of the crowed, one of the smaller children began to cry. Mrs Taylor checked her watch.

"If he's got all that food," began one of the disgruntled mothers, "it makes you wonder what else he's been holding back on."

"What do you mean asked another?"

"Well, there's been all kinds of collections and stuff."

"Did you hear that, Harold? The union has been holding back the raffle money as well!"

Mrs Taylor looked round at the waiting crowd and smiled nervously before checking her watch again.

"Perhaps they've broken down," suggested Janet.

"No, they would have rung," said Sue.

The crowd waited patiently and the small child at the back stopped crying.

"Perhaps we could all sing a song whilst we wait for Santa," suggested Mrs Taylor. "Would you like that children?"

"That's it. I'm going in chuffin' side," said Janet. She was in the process of doing when she was called back by Sue.

"Wait, he's here." Sue was pointing out a blue van that had pulled into the school's drive.

Some of the parents were waving and encouraging the children to do the same.

The van stopped at the entrance to the school's assembly hall about twenty metres away. A prison guard climbed out of the passenger seat and disappeared around the rear of the van, reappearing moments letter (to the delight of the waiting crowd) with Santa.

Santa slung his sack over his shoulder and waved the best he could to the crowd.

One little boy looked up to his mother and asked, "Why is Santa handcuffed to that policeman?"

"They're just protecting the presents," said Mrs Taylor reassuringly.

Santa turned his back on the crowd and set off towards the entrance of the assembly hall.

The minute his back turned; an epidemic of laughter broke out amongst the crowd. Lenny turned to look back, his long white beard covering the look of bewilderment on his face. People had been reacting this way ever since he had left the gymnasium changing rooms. What's wrong with everyone? Lenny asked himself. As he stood there trying to work out what was so funny, he noticed Sue, who was pointing at the sack on his back.

Lenny put it down and examined it. "You bastard Taffy!" he exclaimed, starting to beat at the writing that had been chalked on his sack.

When the word had disappeared, Lenny waved at the crowd again and resumed his journey to the assembly hall.

A little girl looked up at her mother who was still giggling. "What does 'swag' mean mummy?"

Mr Turner and Mr Phillips waited patiently in the wings. Lenny sat on the stage in front of his grotto and greeted the children one by one with a cheery 'ho ho ho' and a present. An occasional feeling of awkwardness came over him whenever one of the children was presented to him by one of his work mates, but, on the whole, he was enjoying the experience.

"Here," said one of the mothers as she placed her child on Lenny's lap, "tell Santa what you want for Christmas." The woman looked at Lenny and quickly added. "Keep you eye on him will you. I've just caught him throwing trifle at Jenny Marsden's little girl. I'd better get her cleaned up before the teachers see her!"

The woman hurried down the steps at the base of the stage and disappeared amongst the hoards of children who were gathered around tables filled with crumpled cakes, demolished buns and untouched sandwiches.

"Well," said Lenny. "You're a big fellow. How old are you?"

The boy looked up at Lenny and attempted to tug his beard.

"I said how old are you big fellow?"

The boy held up five fingers.

"Five, aye, and what's your name?"

"Matthew. What's yours?"

"I'm Santa Claus."

The boy surveyed Lenny for a moment. "No, you're not."

"Yes, I am. What would you like for Christmas?"

"If you were really Santa, you would know! How old i am" the boy took another tug at Lenny's beard.

"Stop doing that," said Lenny, momentarily dropped his deep voice. "Santa knows what you want," he added under his breath.

"What then?" asked the boy as he tried to look under the beard.

"A... bike?"

The boy shook his head.

"A football?"

The boy shook his head.

"A football... shirt, I mean boots?"

"You're a rubbish Santa," said the boy. "The one in Woolworth's is better than you and he's a Paki!"

Lenny raised his finger. "Oy! Do you want me to tell your mother you've been using words like that?"

The boy shrugged his shoulders. "Can I have my present now?"

Lenny took out a present from a sack on his right which was labelled 'boys'. The boy snatched the present from his hand and immediately began to unwrap it.

"Oy!" said Lenny as he snatched it back. "Not until Christmas day."

"But I want to have a look at it."

"Not till Christmas Day," reiterated the boy's mother as she climbed the steps onto the stage. "I hope he's been behaving."

"Yes, he's a little... gem," said Lenny, handing back the present and congratulating himself for not using the word Twat,

The woman grabbed her son's arm and ushered him towards the steps. "I'm so glad, he gave that Paki in Woolworth's a hell of a time!"

If Lenny was pleased to watch the mother and son walk off the stage and down the steps, it was nothing to how he felt when he noticed Sue and Lisa waiting patiently at the base of them.

Sue smiled a warm smile as she approached. Lisa, however, seemed a little nervous.

"Come here and sit on Santa's knee," said Lenny in his best Santa voice.

Lisa looked up at her mother for reassurance.

"Go on," said Sue. "Santa's made a lot of effort to come and see you."

Lenny helped his daughter onto his knee. "Well," he said, trying to disguise his voice even more, "you must be Lisa."

Lisa smiled and looked at her mother in amazement.

"I know that because you are at the top of the list in my, 'who's been good book', added Lenny.

Lisa smiled, shyly but proud.

"If you carry on being a good girl for your mum, I'm going to bring you lots of nice presents. Do you think you can be a good girl till Christmas?"

Lisa nodded her head.

"I'm sure she will be, Santa," said Sue. "She's a very good and loving person…" Sue paused for a moment before adding, "just like her father."

Lenny didn't know what to say, he only knew he wanted to hug his wife and daughter and never let go. It wasn't until he felt a tear in his eye that he knew he had better take control of himself.

"Well then, what would you like for Christmas?"

"Well," Lisa began, who had become overly interested in Santa's hand. "I would like a bike."

Lenny felt his heart sink, he had forgotten about the bike. "Well… I…" he looked at Sue who to his surprise was still smiling.

"I think she deserves a bike," said Sue.

"You do? I mean, bikes are hard to come by, even for Santa."

"I'm sure Santa will be able to find a bike from somewhere."

"You are?" said Lenny with astonishment. Sue nodded her head. "Well, a bike it is then!" said Lenny.

"Did you hear that, mummy? Santa's going to get me a bike."

Sue nodded her head and looked towards the bottom to the steps. A queue had begun to form, and Sue indicated this to Lenny.

"Well, before you go," said Lenny, "I have a little present for you." He leaned over and took out a present from the 'girls' sack.

"Thank you, Santa," said Lisa kissing him on the cheek and climbing down from his knee. "Santa…" said Lisa slowly.

"Yes?"

"The other thing I want for Christmas is my daddy to come home."

Lisa looked at Sue who shrugged her shoulders. "I'm sure he will."

Lisa leaned over and once more kissed Santa on the cheek, but this time whispered something in his ear, "I like your tattoo."

Lenny watched as his wife and daughter walked off the stage, and then looked down at the back of his own hand and at the tattoo that read, 'Sue'.

Taffy and Numbnuts were watching the early evening news and did not notice Lenny's return.

"What's on?" said Lenny as he sat on the end of the couch in front of the TV.

"Hey up," said Numbnuts enthusiastically. "Everything go alright?"

"Yeah, ok."

"Did you see Sandra?"

"No, I don't think she was there. Nice one with the sack Taff."

"Yeah, we were pissing ourselves, wa'n't we Danny?"

"Yeah. Perhaps she was in the kitchens helping out."

"Could have been. Anyway, I didn't see her. Saw our Lisa thought. I think our Susan's got her a bike from somewhere."

"Nice."

"Yeah, great that is."

Lenny detected a hint of jealousy from his two friends. It was something he hadn't expected but could understand. "What's on telly?"

"News," said Numbnuts.

"Owt happened?"

"Nah, not really. Them IRA blokes have gone to trial, talks have broke down with the NUM and the government... oh yeah, if you've got any one-pound notes you'd better spend them before the end of the year."

"Why's that then?"

"That's when they stop being legal tender."

"I thought they already had."

"Me too. Did you look in any of the classrooms?"

"No why?"

Numbnuts seemed a little disheartened. "Just thought she might have been helping out in one of them."

"How come talks keep breaking down?" asked Taffy.

"Because we're on the ropes and the government knows it. We're beaten," said Lenny.

"Funny," said Taffy, "I don't feel beaten."

"I do," said Numbnuts softly.

"Me too," added Lenny.

Chapter Eight

The Home Coming, and Old Bill's Stamp

Janet and Sue were sitting on Janet's sofa quietly drinking tea. Janet took a long hard draw on her cigarette before stubbing it out. "It went alright; I think the kids enjoyed it."

"So do I," agreed Sue

"What went alright?" asked Jim as he passed through the room on his way to the stairs,

"The kid's party."

"Oh yeah, I'd forgotten about that. Did it go alright?"

"I just said it chuffin' did, didn't I?" said Janet raising her voice in mid-sentence as Jim left the room and went upstairs.

"I thought your Lenny was wonderful."

"Yeah. Do you know, I was really proud of him."

"Yeah, not many blokes are like that; selfish pigs most of them!" said Janet this time raising her voice to a shout and directing it to the stairs.

"Still haven't...sorted things?" asked Sue.

"What, with him? No, I've given up on him."

"Well," said Sue sympathetically, "it looks like the strike's crumbling. They'll be back at work soon and maybe we can all get back to normal."

"What will you do? Will you go back to college?"

"Dunno. We'll need to get a bit of money together first."

Jim pounded back downstairs and through the living room. "What's this?" he said on his way through. "You silly old bugger."

Sue looked up at and saw Jim was holding a cucumber in one hand whilst trying to fasten his shirt buttons with the other.

"Found it in't bedroom drawer." Jim slipped on his shoes and carried on to the kitchen (he seemed to be in quite a rush).

Sue heard the fridge door open and close again before Jim came back into the room, pulling on his coat on the way.

"Honestly, she gets worse she does!" Jim bent over the back of the sofa and kissed his wife on the cheek. "Going a bit senile she is. She put a bottle of milk int oven last week. I thought that was bad enough, but a cucumber int dressing table drawer, what were you thinking? Well, I'm off now, see you Sue love."

Jim disappeared back into the kitchen and a few seconds later there was the sound of the back door closing.

Janet and Sue sat in awkward silence. Janet nervously wrapping her neck chain around her finger. Sue put down her cup and saucer and sat quietly for a moment before speaking. "What did you think of the sandwiches?"

The 21st of December took twice as long as the 20th had done, and the 22nd took longer still. There must have been at least fifty-six hours in the 23rd of December, or at least that was how it had seemed to Lenny, but finally Christmas Eve and the day of their release had arrived.

The door to Lenny's cell was opened by one of the guards, which meant it was 8am. Lenny, Numbnuts and Taffy were due to be released at 10am (approximately six hours in prison time). Lenny made his way to the dining room for breakfast. Numbnuts went to use up the last of the credit on his phone card.

"Where's Numbnuts?" asked Taffy.

"He's gone to phone Sandra," answered Lenny as he sat himself down at the table.

"What for? He'll be seeing her in a couple of hours."

Lenny didn't answer he just poked his sausage with his fork and decided he wasn't hungry after all. "Perhaps he wants to remind her he's coming home today; you know to save the embarrassment."

"What are you talking about Taffy?"

"He's been in here for a fortnight now, perhaps he wants to make sure nobody's... you know, stepped into his shoes."

"Like who?" asked Lenny although he somehow knew what Taffy's answer would be.

"Oh... I don't know... someone with a white coat for instance."

Lenny slammed his fork on to the table shattering it and sending white plastic splinters spinning off into his breakfast. "Look, if you've got owt to say, say it"

"I'm not saying anything me."

Lenny pushed his plate away and sat back into his chair, angry with himself for secretly suspecting the same thing as Taffy. It was then he noticed Charlie Marshall sitting at a nearby table and remembered something.

"Look, I'll see you in a minute," said Lenny.

"Yeah. Can I have that sausage?"

Lenny sat himself down in front of Charlie and awaited a response but there was none forthcoming. "Haven't seen much of you lately," he eventually said.

Charlie looked up. "No," he said quietly and returned to his breakfast.

"You bin ill, have you?"

"Yes, you could say that," replied Charlie, this time without looking up.

A silence fell, and Lenny got the feeling Charlie wished to be left alone. Lenny reached into his shirt pocket and produced a letter with a large orange stamp on the front. He slid it across the table towards Charlie.

"Here, you left this in the telly room. I've got the chess set in my cell. I'll make sure you get it back before I leave."

Charlie remained silent. He looked at the letter for a few moments but did not touch it. Then he returned to his breakfast and the silence resumed.

"Well," said Lenny as he rose from his chair. "Like I say, I'll make sure you get the chess set back." Lenny pushed the chair back under the table and turned to leave.

"Did you read it?" said Charlie, stopping Lenny dead in his tracks.

"No, of course I didn't!" Lenny replied, offended at the question.

Charlie gave Lenny a long hard look as if weighing him up. Then, as he began to shake his head ever so slightly, he said, "No, you haven't, have you?"

"Course not," reiterated Lenny, sitting down once more. "Why would I?" Charlie smiled.

"Most people in here would have read it, because most people are like you. Yet... you didn't read it."

"No," Lenny watched as Charlie picked up the letter and put it into his pocket. "What do you mean most people are like me?"

"Most people are interested in my business because most people are interested in the money." Charlie was looking hard into Lenny's face as if daring him to deny it.

"Then you do have the money?" asked Lenny.

"Charlie's smile grew bigger. "Maybe."

"But you're not going to tell anymore than that, are you?"

"I will tell you one thing," said Charlie, leaning over the table in order to speak more quietly. "Never give up your queen!"

Three hours later the prison van pulled up outside the front door of 52, Nelson Road. Mr Turner opened the back doors, and Lenny, Taffy and Numbnuts emerged.

Mr Turner wished them all the best, before climbing back into the van and driving off.

"Well," said Lenny. "We're home." He observed a gang of kids at the end of the road chasing a younger kid who was whirling a dead cat above his head.

Numbnuts took a moment to enjoy the fresh air, "Yeah."

"Well, I'm off for a pint."

"Aren't you going to have a shower or something first?" asked Numbnuts.

Taffy raised his hands in the air and tried to smell his own armpits (this has started to become a habit with Taffy) "I don't smell that bad, do I?"

"Yes," both Numbnuts and Lenny agreed.

"You haven't showered for two weeks!" added Lenny.

Taffy thought for a moment. "Perhaps I'll have a quick one first."

"What? Shower?"

"No, pint!" Taffy set off towards the nearest pub.

"Well," Numbnuts opened his garden gate, "I'll see you tonight, yeah?"

"No, I don't think so," answered Lenny. "I think I'll have a night in. I've been missing our Lisa, you know?"

"Yeah," said Numbnuts sympathetically. "I'll see you tomorrow."

Numbnuts closed the gate behind him and set off down the garden path whilst Lenny crossed the road to his own house.

Lenny reached his own gate and stopped. An old man walking up the road had caught his attention by waving his stick. Lenny impatiently awaited the old man's arrival.

The man eventually completed his short journey and leant forward on his walking stick, giving out a long hard cough.

"Hello Bill," said Lenny with a smile.

Bill took a deep breath. "I'm glad I've caught you. Your Sue said you would be out today."

"Yeah, we've just been dropped off."

"Here, I've got something to show you." Bill searched through his pockets, eventually producing an envelope. He pulled out a photograph and presented it to Lenny.

"It's our Betty," said Bill proudly.

Lenny looked at the photograph of a couple in their early fifties, who were smiling and cutting a wedding cake.

"Yes, that's smashing that is Bill. When did she get married?"

"Last week. Here, look, I've got some more." Bill pulled some more photographs from the envelope. "Do you want to see them?"

Lenny did not want to appear rude, but he was in rather a rush to see his wife and daughter. "Actually, Bill, could I see them some other time? I haven't seen our Lisa or Susan yet?"

Bill looked a little uneasy as he shoved the photographs away. "I'm sorry. You said didn't you, you've only just arrived and here I am keeping you from your family. Don't let me keep you any longer. Go on, I'll show you another day." Bill gave out a loud cough and set off up the road. "Merry Christmas."

Lenny smiled as he bid Bill a Merry Christmas back and then set off up his path, pausing for a moment at his front door before opening it and stepping inside.

"Honey," shouted Lenny, "I'm home."

Lisa came tearing down the hallway and wrapped her arms around her father's legs. She was closely followed by his wife who wrapped her arms around his neck.

Lenny tried to take a step back to counterbalance the weight of bodies that now engulfed him, but he found he could not. Within seconds, he found himself flat on his back with his wife and daughter on top. Sue rolled to one side and roared with laughter. Lisa, who was also in hysterics, climbed onto his chest and threw her arms around her father's neck. Lenny, realising everyone was all right, began to laugh too. It was something he hadn't done for a long time, and he was finding it hard to stop. Eventually, the laughter subsided just enough for Lenny to speak. "Did anyone miss me?" and the laughter erupted once more.

Christmas morning was all that Lenny had expected and more. He was awoken, at 6:30 in the morning, by Lisa jumping up and down on his bed. He and Sue watched their daughter open her presents, then Lenny took Lisa to the park where he taught her to ride (almost), her brand new pink bike. Now, after such a busy morning, Lenny found himself ready for a nap. Lisa was upstairs playing with her dollhouse; Sue was in the kitchen preparing dinner and so Lenny decided to lie on the sofa and close his eyes for ten minutes. Lenny's undirected thoughts took him back to the day he had sat on stage dressed in a Santa's outfit with his daughter kissing him on the cheek and whispering, "I like your tattoo!"

Lenny wondered if Lisa had recognised him or was it just a coincidence. She was a very perceptive little girl, and she did seem to be growing up very quickly thought Leny. Perhaps his little girl was a little older and wiser than he had given her credit for.

Lenny had just drifted off to sleep when a knock at the front door startled him back into semi-consciousness. "I'll get that," he shouted, dragging himself up off the sofa.

Lenny stretched some life back into himself as he opened the front door and was surprised to be confronted by the awesome figure of a man in a black suit.

Lenny rubbed the sleep from his eyes and looked again.

"Levi, what are you doing here?"

Levi smiled. "Heavy night last night?"

"No, I er... I didn't go out."

"Thought you would have, first day back and all that. How you doin?"

"Not so bad," said Lenny trying to peer over Levi's enormous shoulders at two more large men in suits, who seemed to be hovering around the van that was parked outside his front gate.

"How are you?"

"Oh, I'm doing great. Never did get the chance to thank you though."

"Thank me, what for?"

"The advice you gave me, you know, about packing in at pit and starting a new career."

Lenny thought for a few seconds and then remembered the day outside the 'Miner's institute'.

"Oh that. All turned out alright, did it?"

"Yes, great, business is booming. I'm getting loads of overtime. Best move I ever made, can't thank you enough."

Lenny looked again at the two men who were now hovering around his garden gate.

"What is it exactly you do now?"

"I'm a repo man." Levi looked slightly uncomfortable as he spoke.

"What do you mean a repo man?" asked Lenny cautiously.

"I collect things; you know thigs that people haven't made payments on."

"Oh," said Lenny who thought this was a far from honourable profession. "No wonder business is booming, what with strike an' all."

"Yes, every cloud has a silver lining," said Levi as he tried to force a laugh.

An awkward silence fell. Eventually Lenny spoke again. "Well, it's been nice talking to you. Perhaps I'll see you later."

Lenny began to close the door, but it was stopped by Levi's enormous hand.

"Actually Lenny, its not a social visit. It's about your telly."

A few seconds later, Lenny was laying flat on his back looking up at Levi who was sitting on his chest. He stopped kicking and screaming in order to catch his breath.

"I'm sorry about this," said Levi.

"Sorry! What do you mean you're fuckin' sorry?" screamed Lenny as he engaged in another fruitless attempt to break free.

"Well, you know, you bein' a mate an' all."

The two men in black suits stepped over Lenny being very careful not to drop the telly. This was very difficult as Sue and a frying pan were impeding their progress.

Levi waited until Sue and the men had passed. "Listen," he said quietly, "I was supposed to take your video recorder as well, but I'm going to leave that for another week."

"What goods a fuckin' video recorder without a fuckin' telly you fat oaf?" screamed Lenny.

"Well… haven't you got a portable?"

Lenny didn't answer he was too busy kicking his legs and flailing his arms.

Suddenly Sue reappeared and started beating Levi about the head with her frying pan.

Levi raised his hands to protect himself. "Leave off, Sue."

"Get off him you fat bastard!" screamed Sue. "You ought to be ashamed of yourself. Why are you doing this? It's Christmas day you know?"

"Yes, I was telling Lenny here that I'm getting some overtime in, treble time you know."

Levi slowly climbed up from Lenny's chest and walked out of the front door, fending off the occasion blow from Sue. Lenny darted off into the living room. Sue ceased her onslaught at the bottom of the garden path and allowed Levi to leave with no further impediment, save verbal abuse.

Suddenly, there was a loud crash. Levi looked round to see several pieces of a video recorder skidding towards him.

"Here, take your fuckin' video," shouted Lenny from the front door.

Levi turned back and opened his arms slightly as if to make amends, but the raising of Sue's frying pan made him change his mind.

Levi climbed into the van and drove off down the street, leaving Lenny and Sue in stunned silence on the doorstep, until Sue noticed the attention being paid by the neighbours.

"What are you staring at?" she shouted to a passer-by who had stopped passing by.

"Think it's funny, do you?" The passer-by resumed passing by.

Sue followed her husband into the house and firmly slammed the door behind her.

It was December 28th and Father O'Connor was sitting quietly in the confession booth reading his Bible. As he marked down various chapters that he thought might be helpful in his Sunday service, he heard the adjoining door open then close again. He closed his book and waited patiently.

"Forgive me father for I have sinned," came a voice from the next booth. Then after a brief silence the voice added, "well... least... I think I chuffin' have... sorry father, I mean, I think I may have sinned."

Father O'Connor was slightly taken back by this remark. It wasn't the swearing that shocked him, (preaching in a mining community that was something he was used to), it was the fact that the person in the other booth did not appear to know whether they had sinned or not!

"You say you are not sure if you have sinned or not. That surprises and shocks me. Do you not know the Bible?"

"Oh yes," replied the voice. "I mean, I've sort of sinned... I think."

"I think you had better explain," said Father O'Connor in a quiet voice. There was a long silence as the person in the other booth thought deeply.

"Well, I've been thinking of being unfaithful to my husband... you know... in a sexual way."

Father O'Connor looked shocked and confused. "And you don't know if that's a sin! The good book speaks out on infidelity many times. It even speaks out against it in the Ten Commandments given to Moses on Mount Sinai. THOU SHALL

NOT COMMIT ADULTERY. This means a woman who has entered into the sanctity of marriage BEFORE GOD will stay FAITHFUL TO HIM FORSAKING ALL OTHERS. So how can you tell me you do not now if you have sinned? You must know it is a sin to have sexual relations with any man other than your husband!"

"I do father, I do," replied the voice, "but what does the good book say about...fruit and veg?"

Janet, Jim, Sandra, Numbnuts and Sue sat at their usual table at the back of the concert room, patiently waiting for Lenny to return with the drinks.

"What was it like in prison?" asked Jim.

"Well, it was a bit scary at first. There was this big bloke called Bill the axe!" Numbnuts thought for a moment. "Or was it Bob the axe? Anyway, he was called summat the axe, and they called him that because he killed his neighbours for having their telly on too loud."

Jim looked shocked. "Really, how did he do it?"

"Do what?" asked Numbnuts.

"You know, how did he kill 'em?"

"Well... with an axe... that's why they call him 'the axe'."

"Right."

"And, there was this other bloke called Norman."

"Don't tell me, Norman the knife."

"No, just Norman."

"Oh right. What was he in for?" Jim sounded a little disappointed.

"Nonpayment of fines."

"Right," Jim looked a lot disappointed. "Tell me about Bill the axe man."

"Well," started Numbnuts.

"Will you two shut up about prison," interjected Janet. "Honestly, its all a big adventure to you lot. What about these two?" Janet pointed at Sue and Sandra. "They've been worried sick and probably want to forget whole thing, but you two have talked about nowt else all chuffin week!"

An uneasy silence fell over the table that was only broken by Lenny returning with a tray of drinks. He noticed the silence to which he had returned the sheepish looks on Jim and

Numbnuts' faces and decided to break the mood. "Hey, did we tell you who we met in prison?"

Janet folded her arms, Sue hung her head, Sandra sat back in er chair and Jim and Numbnuts became even more sheepish.

"Suit yourselves," said Lenny taking a sip of his larger.

"Bingo tickets are on sale at the Bingo booth, bingo will be starting in five minutes. Bingo tickets at the Bingo booth," said a voice over the microphone.

Janet rummaged around in her handbag before presenting her husband with a fifty pence piece. "Here, go and get me a couple of tickets."

"I'm not wasting money on bloody bingo!" protested Jim pocketing the fifty pence.

"Go on then," said Janet angrily, "just deny me my last little pleasure."

Jim reluctantly stood up. "Anybody else want one while I'm there?"

Sue and Sandra each slid coins across the table.

"I'll have one."

"I'll have two."

Jim set off towards the queue at the bingo booth.

"What are we doing for New Years Eve?" asked Numbnuts.

"Don't know," replied Lenny as he pulled out his tobacco tin. "If this lot keep wasting money on bingo tickets we won't be going anywhere."

"Oh, stop your bloody moaning," said Sue, "Has anyone got a pen?"

"Only I thought we could go to fancy dress," continued Numbnuts.

Lenny stopped rolling his cigarette. "What fancy dress?"

"There's a fancy dress party on in here, New Years Eve."

"That's a good idea," interrupted Sandra, "that'll be a right laugh."

"I don't know, it's a lot of messing about," said Lenny.

"Not for you," suggested Sue, who seemed to be keen on the idea. "You could wear your Santa outfit."

"Yeah," agreed Sandra. "We could make it a Christmas theme. I could go as Mary and I could do that with some old bed sheets."

"I'll be an angel," said Sue. "What are you going to be, Janet?"

"Hold on, hold on," interrupted Lenny. "Does this fancy dress thing cost owt to get in?"

"No, it's free and there's a prize for the winner," said Numbnuts excitedly.

"So, what are you going to be?" repeated Sue.

"Taffy chuffin Owen!" said Janet and everyone realised Janet was looking elsewhere.

"Anybody sitting here?" asked Taffy as he pulled out a chair and almost missed sitting on it.

"Where's Jim?"

It was painfully obvious to Janet that Taffy had had a little too much to drink.

"He's gone for some bingo tickets, and that's his seat."

"Bingo?" Taffy screwed up his face and ignored the fact he had just taken someone's seat. "You're not playing bingo, are you?"

"Women are!" answered Numbnuts.

"What's up with a game of Bingo?" asked Janet.

"It's boring."

"Well, if you don't like it, you can go in't other side and drink your pint."

"What and miss BINGO?" said Taffy sarcastically before turning to address Lenny.

"Bill's looking for you." Taffy glanced back at Janet and was pleased to see her angry.

"What for?"

"Dunno, dint say."

"Hey up," said a voice from behind Taffy. "You're in my seat!"

Taffy stood up and let Jim sit down.

"It's all right, I was just going, don't want to sit here and listen to BINGO." Taffy threw a glance at Janet before leaving.

Everyone informed Jim of their decision regarding the fancy dress, everyone that is except Lenny whose attention was elsewhere.

He had noticed something odd. Taffy had not (as expected) left in the directed of the other room, or the bar. Instead, he had gone to the front of the room where he was hanging around the Bingo machine in a very suspicious manner.

The Bingo machine consisted of a large glass case, containing a number of coloured ping-pong balls, all of which were numbered, at the top of the box was a ten-inch Perspex tube for the balls to make their exit once the machine was switched on. At the top of the Perspex tube was a wire bent into a semicircle designed to hold the first ball in place allowing other balls to form a queue behind it.

Taffy hung around for a few minutes until the man sitting behind the box turned his back in order to retrieve a microphone. Quick as a flash Taffy leaned over the box, and within a couple of seconds had returned to his standing-around-looking innocent pose.

Taffy left the Bingo machine and passed Lenny's table on his way to the bar, casting a wink at Lenny as he did so.

"Good luck with the Bingo, Janet," said Taffy as he passed.

Janet ignored him as usual.

"Right, eyes down for your first number," said the man behind the Bingo machine.

Everyone looked down at their tickets, pens at the ready, and the machine was switched on.

The balls inside started flying around in all different directions. Almost immediately, the first ball found the opening at the top, leading to the Perspex tube. The ball entered and accelerated up, but instead of stopping at the top as it should, the ball carried on and was fired twenty feet into the air, closely followed by a second and a third. The man in charge of the machine jumped up in a futile attempt to catch the now rapidly descending ping-pong balls; in his panic, he didn't think to turn off the machine. Within a few seconds, the balls were all bouncing off tables and ricocheting off walls. One even found its way into Jim's pint pot.

A close examination of the machine would later reveal that the wire at the top of the Perspex tube, designed to stop and hold the balls in place, had been bent to one side by person or persons unknown.

Lenny and a great number of other men were laughing loudly. He looked at Taffy who was quietly drinking at the bar and discreetly gave him a 'thumbs up' sign.

Colin sat looking out of the window of his father's old car, as he waited at the lights at the bottom of the hill. He had not realised how much the village had grown since he was a boy. Behind the lights of his own village, in the distance, were the lights of an entire city, covering two very large hills. These lights were the lights of Sheffield, and beyond them, still more lights. As Colin gazed at the vastness of the lights, he was aware that for every light he could see there was a person, or even a family using it. Millions of lights serving millions of people.

Colin Vine felt very, very insignificant.

He opened the car door, and with some difficulty stood up. With one foot in plaster and the other sporting two broken toes he had found it difficult driving, but he needed the car; it was essential to his plan.

Colin closed the door and hobbled to the boot, which he promptly opened. The boot was dark, its interior bulb had long since burnt out, so Colin felt his way around, leaning into the boot until he came across the object he had placed there earlier.

Colin struggled to haul himself upright again on his damaged limbs and gave himself a boost by pushing with his hands against the boot's carpeted bottom.

Holding the object he had retrieved high in the air, as if to illuminate it with lights from the village. Colin stared up at the length of hosepipe in his hand as if it were a trophy, a trophy he deserved. He took one end of the hose and knelt on the ground. All he had to do was to put one end in the car's exhaust and the other through the window. Then he could simply sit back in the car and watch the lights, and soon all his troubles would be over.

If Colin was baffled by the absence of the exhaust protruding out from the back of the car, he was even more baffled by the absence of the back of the car.

He looked up in horror at the car that was gently rolling away from him, down a hill, that was getting steeper by the metre.

He did not know whether he had left the handbrake off, or whether the handbrake simply didn't work. He did, however, know that his final push from the boot had set off a chain of events, which if he could not stop them, would have dire consequences, and would ruin his attempt at suicide!

Colin struggled to his feet and hobbled as best as he could after the car. Just for a moment, Colin thought he might catch it, but, as if to taunt him, the moment he was about to lay hands on it, the car pulled away, gaining speed as the hill got steeper.

Colin stopped hobbling and watched the car as it veered off the road and disappeared over the hillside.

He wondered if he could perhaps climb down the hill, maybe the engine would still work. Yes, that was all he needed to do.

Suddenly, there was a flash of light and a sound of a large explosion from the bottom of the hill. Colin watched as the car, along with his plan, went up in smoke.

Lenny sat on his sofa watching the afternoon news on an old black and white TV borrowed from Numbnuts. He took a sip of his cheep lager.

"That must be terrible," said Numbnuts, who was sitting next to him nursing a can of his own.

Sue glanced up briefly from her sewing, and pricked her finger,

"I hope I never get like that," continued Numbnuts.

The news story was covering some old peoples home and its impending closure. "What, old?" said Lenny.

"Well, no, not old. I don't mind living till I'm sixty or something, but I hope I don't get like them."

"Has Sandra finished her costume?" asked Sue who was getting fed up with what she considered to be a depressing conversation.

"Yes, she finished it yesterday." Numbnuts took a sip from his can and watched some more TV. "If I ever got like that, I think I'd top myself," he continued a moment later.

"What time did she have to be at clinic?"

"Ten o'clock... it can't be much of a life sat in a nursing home all day watching telly."

"I know what you mean," agreed Lenny. "You know what I can't stand?"

Numbnuts shook his head. "What?"

"Not being able to do owt for myself."

Lenny and Numbnuts watched a little more, occasionally shaking their heads until Lenny realised that his can was empty. "Get us two more lagers out of fridge, pet." Lenny passed Sue his empty.

Sue put down her sewing and begrudgingly went to the kitchen, returning moments later with two fresh cans.

"Do you know," said Lenny. "I sometimes think they should allow euthanasia."

"Yeah," agreed Numbnuts before asking. "What's that?"

"It's when you are allowed to take your own life or... your mate's life... you know before you become a burden on others."

"I'd agree with that." Numbnuts thought for a moment. "Would you kill me... you know, if I became a burden?"

"I suppose, if you asked me to."

Numbnuts smiled appreciatively. "Cheers mate. I'd kill you an' all."

Suddenly, there was a knock at the back door. Sue looked at Lenny and Numbnuts, Lenny and Numbnuts looked at Sue. Sue eventually rose to her feet and threw her sewing into the chair. "I'll get it, shall I?"

Lenny and Numbnuts listened to the muffled voices at the back door and noted a long hard cough amidst the conversation. Sue returned followed by Bill.

"Hey up, Bill," said Lenny moving along the settee and allowing Bill to be seated.

Sue returned to her seat and her sewing.

"I was just passing," said Bill, "so I thought I'd pop in."

"Any time. Would you like a drink?"

"Don't mind if I do," said Bill before coughing.

"Sue love, go and get Bill a drink."

"How are you, Bill?" asked Numbnuts politely.

"Can't complain," said Bill with another lung-busting cough.

"Hey," said Lenny with a false smile, "you 'ant got them photos of your sister's wedding, have you? Sue... Bill... a drink!"

Sue, whose angry looks had gone unnoticed, once more rose to her feet and, after throwing her sewing down, headed, yet again, to the kitchen.

"As it happens," said Bill, "I've got them here."

Bill pulled out the envelope and handed Lenny half a dozen photographs.

Lenny looked at the pictures one by one, making sure he commented on each before passing them onto Numbnuts.

"Is that your sister?" asked Numbnuts pointing to one of the pictures and holding it up to Bill.

"Yeah, that's our Betty."

Numbnuts handed the photographs back, and Bill was about to put them away, when Sue re-entered the room.

"Don't put them away; I haven't seen them yet." Sue traded a can of lager for the photographs and sat back in her seat.

"Ah, aren't they lovely? I don't think I know your sister. Betty did you say?"

"Yeah, Betty. No, you wouldn't, she dint live in't village, she lived..." Bill broke into another bout of coughing, "...over t'hill. She used to visit me once a week."

"Long way for her to come now, eh Bill," interjected Numbnuts, who immediately wished he hadn't.

"Yeah." Bill took a drink from his can.

"Anyway, they're lovely," said Sue as she handed back the photographs.

"What are you doing tonight, Bill?" asked Lenny. "There's a fancy dress on down at club."

"Oh ah, I'd look alright in fancy bloody dress. Who would I go as? Old Father time?" Bill took another drink of his lager. "I don't know, I might go down just to watch you lot make idiots of yourselves!" Bill took a final drink and rose to his feet. "Anyway, I better get off. Thanks for the drink."

"That's alright, Bill, anytime. See you Bill."

"Yes, see you later, Bill," added Numbnuts.

Bill set off towards the back door.

"I'll see him out, shall I?" said Sue sharply, following Bill into the kitchen.

"What's up with her?" asked Numbnuts.

Lenny shrugged his shoulders. "Dunno. Want another drink?"

"Go on then."

"SUSAN!"

Lenny sat on the sofa rolling a cigarette. He was taking extra care so as not to get tobacco on his Santa costume. He looked at his watch and went to the foot of the stairs.

"Come on, we're going to be late," he shouted before returning to the room.

Lenny put a cigarette in his mouth, picked up his lighter and held it to the end of his badly rolled cig, but then stopped. He took off his large white beard and threw it on the sofa, and then he struck up the lighter and lit his cigarette. He looked at his watch again and sat down, growing more and more impatient.

It was five past eight and they were supposed to call at Janet and Jim's house at eight.

Lenny, who didn't fancy walking into the club in fancy dress to find out no one else had bothered, was beginning to wonder if Janet and Jim would wait.

"Come on Sue, it's five past," he shouted.

"Nearly ready," came a muffled voice from upstairs.

Lenny pulled out the long white beard he had inadvertently sat on, and which had started working its way down the back of the sofa and out popped an envelope. The envelope had obviously slipped down the back of the sofa at some point and Lenny was curious as to what it contained.

He held the envelope up in the air and shook it: nothing. He looked inside: nothing.

Perhaps it had once contained a Christmas card he thought, turning it over to read the back.

MR W. MURPHY
21 MAPLE AVENUE
MALTON S. YORKSHIRE
ENGLAND.

Lenny knew straight away who Mr W Murphy was, that was Bill. It must be the envelope that had contained Bill's photographs. He had obviously dropped it during his visit earlier in the day.

Lenny was about to discard the envelope when he noticed something, something strange yet familiar.

Lenny stared at the stamp. It was large, it was orange and it had something in the middle, something that looked like broken eggshells. The stamp was identical to the one he had seen in prison. The one that had been sent to Charlie Marshall.

"What do you think then?" said a voice from the door.

Sue, who often looked like an angel to Lenny, looked like an angel to Leny. She was wearing a long white dress, and springing out from the shoulders were two long white wings.

"That's smashing that is," said Lenny who was secretly more interested in the stamp.

"You've done really well with that. Come here, take a look at this."

Sue sat on the arm of the sofa and peered down at the envelope taking great care to fold her wings to one side as she did so.

"What do you reckon to this?" said Lenny.

"What? It's an envelope?"

"Yes but look at the stamp." Sue took a closer look.

"Oh yes, it's Australian. Bill must've dropped it. Come on, we're late."

"How do you know it's Australian?" asked Lenny.

"It's got a picture of the Sydney Opera House on it!"

Lenny looked at the stamp and the egg like structure. "That's a building?"

"Yeah, it's Sydney Opera House."

Something was bugging Lenny, but he wasn't quite sure what. "Where would you get a stamp like this?" he asked.

"Derrrr! Australia!" answered Sue, in an overly sarcastic manner.

"No, seriously. You couldn't get this stamp from anywhere else?"

"I wouldn't have thought so. Come on, we'd better get going."

As Lenny and Sue walked down the road, Lenny found he could not get rid of a memory, the memory of Charlie Mashall getting up from a table and leaving behind him a chess set and an envelope, and envelope with a big orange stamp.

Chapter Nine

The Fairy, the Angel, the Grim Reaper, the Christmas Tree, Andy Pandy, Santa and the Six-Foot Penis.

Peter Bellis loosened his kipper tie and sat on one of the benches that lined the railway platform. The night air was cold, but Peter was hot, hot and nervous. He looked over his shoulder as a man passed by him and did not take his eyes off him until he disappeared into a cafe at the end of the platform. There were very few people about, but that was how Peter had wanted it. That was why he had chosen New Years Eve.

Peter put his hand in his pocket, pulled out a key and looked around again. He noticed a man on the next platform carrying a briefcase and an umbrella. Peter put the key away and watched the man suspiciously. A woman with a pushchair came out of the cafe but walked off in the opposite direction. Peter turned his attention back to the man with the briefcase, who was doing nothing more than looking at his watch.

After a while, a train arrived at the next platform, the man with the briefcase got on it. A few minutes later the train pulled away and Peter rose from his bench, gripping the key in his pocket tightly and began to walk along the platform. He walked past brightly lit offices and billboards, and approached a sign that said 'LOST LUGGAGE' underneath which was a smaller sign that said 'LOCKERS 1 TO 90'.

He was about to open the door beneath the sign, when he noticed two men walking towards him. Peter walked past the door and kept walking. One of the men, wearing a raincoat, smiled. His friend, in a pin-striped suit, wished Peter a 'Happy New Year' as they passed. Peter forced a smile and a nod and kept walking, until the men's footsteps disappeared into the distance. Peter turned; the platform was empty.

He headed to the locker room door, this time more hurriedly. A small bell above the door sounded as he entered, and a man in railway uniform stood up from behind the lost luggage counter. Peter smiled, held up a key and pointed towards the lockers at the far end of the room. The man behind the counter nodded before sitting back down and reopening his broadsheet.

Peter walked over to the lockers and pulled out a key. The number on the key was 22. He walked along the lockers until he came to a top locker sporting a brass plaque that read 22. His heart was racing, and his hands were sweating so much that he thought he was going to drop the key as he placed it in the lock. He looked around the room one last time before he turned the key and opened the door. Inside a large carrier bag with the letters C&A on the side. He pulled the bag from the locker and peered inside. Everything was just as he had left it. In the bottom of the bag was £20,000 in £20 notes. Peter closed the locker door, tucked the bag under his arm and headed for the exit.

Once again, the bell at the top of the door rang as he opened it. The man behind the counter looked up briefly before returning to his newspaper.

Peter stepped through the door and out onto the platform. He was about to walk away in the direction of the cafe when, to his horror, he noticed two men standing outside it. The man in the pin-striped suit was lighting the cigarette of the man in the raincoat. Peter stepped back into the recess of the doorway and froze. He was just considering slipping back into the locker room when a train slowly came to a halt in front of him. One of the doors opened and out stepped two teenagers, one of whom seemed very drunk. The second of the two, who seemed less drunk, closed the door behind them before taking his friend by the arm and leading him away.

Peter waited, not daring to step out from the recess of the door. After what seemed an eternity, the train began to move. Gripping the C&A bag tightly, Peter dashed across the platform. He opened the door of the moving train and climbed aboard, closing the door behind him, he crouched behind it, keeping himself below the window line and not daring to look out.

Lenny held open the doors to the Miner's Institute's function room for a slightly overweight fairy.

"Thank you," shouted the fairy above the music that had suddenly hit her in the face. She waved her wand at him. "I'll give you three chuffin' wishes for that."

Next through the door was the angel who said, "Get us a brandy chuck; I'm bloody freezing."

Lenny pushed the door a little wider to allow the Christmas tree to gain access.

"I'm not so sure this is a good idea," said the Christmas tree. "I'm never going to be able to get to bar you know."

"That's ok, Jim," replied Lenny. "I'll go to't bar for you."

Santa Claus, the angel, the fairy and the Christmas tree found a spare table at the far end of the room and Santa set off to the bar.

"How did you make your wings?" asked Sue.

Janet turned her shoulders slightly to show her wings. "A pair of tights and a coat hanger," she said with a proud smile. "How did you make yours?"

"Cardboard and felt."

"These anybody's chairs?" asked a gorilla.

"We're saving them for someone," replied Janet and the gorilla headed off in search of chairs.

"How did Sandra get on at clinic?" asked Janet.

"I don't know; she hasn't been round."

Lenny arrived with the drinks. "Here you are," he said passing them around.

"Have you seen owt of Danny and Sandra?" asked Sue.

"Not since this morning love, why?" answered Lenny as he took his first drink wetting his beard in the process.

"No reason."

"Hey up," said Lenny, leaning over the table to Jim, "have you seen Taffy?"

"No," said Jim who was more interested in trying to blow a large red bauble away from his face. "I feel a right tit!"

Lenny laughed. "Wait till you see Taffy."

Janet pointed across the rapidly growing crowd. "There they are."

Everybody looked around, except Jim who was growing increasingly frustrated at the baubles refusal to get out his face.

"Where?" said Sue. "I can't see them."

"There look, they're talking to Sinbad the sailor. Yoo hoo!"

Sandra noticed Janet who was standing and waving. A few minutes later, she and Numbnuts joined the table.

"I like the Virgin Mary costume, Sandra, but what has the Grim Reaper got to do with Christmas?" asked Lenny, as Numbnuts was about to sit down.

"I haven't come as the Grim Reaper," protested Numbnuts. "Do you know you're the third person to think I'm the Grim Reaper!"

"Oh, I'm sorry," said Lenny, who wasn't. "It's the long black cloak and the hood thing that threw me, oh yes and the scythe."

"He's come as Christmas future," explained Sandra.

"You know, from 'Great Expectations'," explained Sandra.

"A Christmas Carol," corrected Sandra.

Lenny felt a little embarrassed at his own ignorance. "Still. I wouldn't go past nursing home on your way home if I were you."

The room got busier, and everyone got drunker. By 11 o'clock, everyone was having a thoroughly good time. Lenny, Jim and Numbnuts were sitting at their table watching their wives dance, when a six-foot penis arrived with four pints.

"Cheers Taffy," said Numbnuts.

"Yeah, thanks Taff."

Lenny didn't say anything; his mind was elsewhere.

"That's last time I'm going t' bar," announced Taffy. "People keep tripping over my testicles." Taffy pushed his testicles under the table and sat down.

"We're having a bit of a do round at our house after, Taff, if you're bothered," announced Jim.

"Thanks Jim, don't mind if I do."

"Just don't tell Janet I told you," added Jim.

Numbnuts, Jim and Taffy sat listening to the music and watching people dance. Lenny sat thinking about a large orange stamp and a man in prison.

"Who's that Andy Pandy dancing with your Sandra?" asked Jim. "It looks like..."

Suddenly, Andy Pandy did a twirl and Jim could see it was Georgio.

"It's our milk man," said Numbnuts who wasn't at all upset. In fact, Numbnuts had been in a curiously good mood all night.

Janet, Sue and Sandra made their way back to the table but didn't sit down.

"You lot dancing or what?" asked Sue as she took a sip of lager.

"What?" said Lenny, who was staring at an old man with a walking stick coughing profusely at a table nearby. "No… I er… I'm just going to talk to old Bill." He got up and left the table.

"Looks like you," said Sue as she took Taffy by the arm.

"What with my balls?" said Taffy. "You must be joking."

"Come on. I'm not getting turned down by two men tonight," insisted Sue pulling Taffy from his seat.

Sue and Taffy set off towards the dancefloor and Taffy fell over his testicles. Sandra and Numbnuts followed them, leaving Janet and Jim alone at the table.

"Are you coming then?" said Janet, in a 'you better be' sort of way.

Jim begrudgingly put down his pint. "Suppose so."

"By the way," said Janet, "I've invited Georgio back tonight. I was a bit rude to him the other day.

"Hello Bill," said Lenny as he sat himself down at Bill's table.

"Hello," Bill replied slowly. "Who are you?"

Lenny took off his beard.

"Lenny, how are you? Have you seen Taffy?" Bill laughed.

"Yeah. Always said he was a prick. Listen Bill, I've been wondering about something. It's about your David."

Bill screwed up his face. "Our David?"

"I was wondering… I know it's a long shot, but does your David know a man called Charlie Marshall?"

Bill immediately looked uncomfortable. "How do you know about Charlie Marshall?"

"I was in prison with him." Lenny waited for Bill to say more, but Bill remained quiet. "Look, Charlie Marshall received a letter from Australia about the same time as you were sent those photographs. With him just living across the way, at Brookly. I thought...your sister..." A thought had just his Lenny like a bomb. "Your sister, she lived at Brookly."

Lenny thought back to the time, just a few weeks ago outside the Institute, the day Bill had offered them the pigeons. They'd been talking about his sister and Numbnuts had said, 'I don't think I know her, do I? Bill replied, 'no, probably not, she used to live across the way in Brookly'.

"And so," continued Lenny slowly, "your David would have lived in Brookly too."

Again, Bill did not answer.

"Look, what's wrong with your David knowing Charlie Marshall? I know Charlie Marshall, so what?"

Lenny could tell he was upsetting Bill, something he hadn't intended to do. Lenny got up and was about to leave when Bill spoke. "He's, his father."

"What?" said Lenny as another memory came racing back. It was the memory of Charlie in the prison dining room, when Lenny had asked the question 'kids?' Charlie had replied, 'a son, David'.

And then, yet another memory. It was when they were talking about Charlie's release, Charlie had said 'I was thinking of emigrating somewhere warm, perhaps making amends with my son, and the rest of my family.' Lenny's head was spinning, and he sat back down.

"It's something we don't like to talk about," said Bill quietly. "You know, having an armed robber for a father."

"I understand," replied Lenny, who was in fact trying to understand a great many things!

"Always a wrong un was Charlie," continued Bill as he gave out a slight cough. That's why our Betty left him, wanted to get as far away from him as she could. Emigrated she did, best thing she could have done too if you ask me. Our David, he moved in with me. He had his exams you see. Charlie wasn't bothered about the boy; it was his wife he couldn't stand to lose."

"Wait a minute," interrupted Lenny. "Charlie married your sister? I thought you meant your sister just had a child to him."

"What are you trying to say about our Betty?"

"Nothing, it's just that I thought Charlie's wife's name was Elizabeth."

"It is Elizabeth, Elizabeth Ann Murphy, at least that's what she was christened, but the family just call her Betty."

Lenny's head was swimming. "But she's dead; Charlie told me his Elizabeth died of cancer. Why would he say that?"

"Look," said Bill, as he rose to his feet. "I don't know what Charlie Marshall told you, but our Betty is alive and well and living in Australia."

"Then why say she was dead?"

"Could be," said Bill as he slipped his coat on, "that he can't face up to the fact that his wife left him. Perhaps he prefers everyone to think she's dead. Could be that he was messing with your head. Anyway, it dunt really matter. Have a good New Year and I'll see you later."

Bill departed, leaving Lenny with his head feeling like a Bingo machine. Thoughts and fragments of conversation bounced around his mind like the machine's ping-pong balls. The trouble being, there was no Perspex tube and bit of wire to allow them to line up in any reasonable order.

After a while, Lenny became aware of someone talking to him.

"Are we or not?" said Numbnuts.

"Are we what?" asked Lenny slowly.

"Are we having another, or are we going back to Jim's house?"

Lenny didn't answer, his mind had once more detached itself from the outside world and memories of his conversations with Charlie were beginning to form some kind of order in his head,

'My wife died three years ago, quite suddenly, cancer. Elizabeth was only forty-nine.'

'A son, David.'

'...Thinking of emigrating.'

'One point two million.'

'Is Father O'Connor still the priest?'

'A bit of everything, gardening mainly.'

'Never give up your queen.'

'I used to work for the Parish Council; I planted the flower beds on the west embankment.'

'Three years ago, cancer.'

Numbnuts sat down and shook Lenny. "Are you alright?"

"She's not dead. Why would he say she's dead, when she's living in Australia?"

"Who's not dead?" asked Numbnuts.

"Elizabeth Ann Marshall," Lenny answered as if his mind was somewhere else.

"Elizabeth Ann Marshall is dead," said Numbnuts confidently.

It took a short time for this information to sink in, but when it did it certainly brought Lenny straight back to the real world. "What... How do you know? Did you know her?"

"No, but I've seen her grave!"

"What?"

"That day you were throwing pigeons at me. You were talking about your Sue wanting to be a teacher. You were standing in front of a grave that said 'Elizabeth Ann Marshall. Born 1932. Died 1981. My..."

"My Queen," interrupted Lenny as the memory of the tombstone returned, turning his legs to jelly, as it brought along another memory. The memory of Charlie Marshall holding up a chess piece in front of Lenny, and saying, 'Never give up your queen'.

Lenny sat in silence. He could not hear Numbnuts asking him if he wanted another drink. He could not even hear the music of the disco. He could only hear the sound of his heartbeat as the blood pumped around his head. Suddenly, Lenny jumped to his feet and pushed his way through the crowd, leaving people wiping their clothes and complaining in his wake.

Lenny reached Bill Murphy, as he was about to open the door leading to the foyer. Lenny spun Bill around. "Bill. Charlie Marshall said he was a gardener for the Parish Council, is that true?"

Bill laughed and coughed. "A gardener? Well, I suppose he did do some gardening in the summer, but his main job for the council was digging graves. He was a grave digger!" Bill turned his back and walked out the door, leaving Lenny frozen at the spot.

Colin Vine carefully climbed the railway embankment. This was not easy with his pot preventing any ankle movement, but he eventually reached the top.

'There is nothing on this earth that could stop a high-speed train at the dead of night', Colin told himself. It would be impossible for the driver to see him until the very last second, and then it would be too late. All he had to do was to find the train lines and wait.

Colin took out a small torch and found the train lines. He stepped between them, put out his torch and waited.

Chapter Ten

Giving up the Queen

After a while, Lenny came out of his coma, walked quietly back to his table and sat down. Thoughts were no longer racing around his head; everything was in order, yet he still did not dare to believe.

Eventually, everyone at the table stopped bickering about whether or not they should have another drink or not.

"What's a matter Chuck?" asked Sue.

Lenny failed to answer, prompting Janet to ask, "Is he alright?"

"I know where the money is," said Lenny still staring at nothing,

"What money? What's he on about?" asked Jim.

"The money Charlie stole. I know where it is."

"Charlie who? What's he talking about?" asked Janet.

"Lenny," said Numbnuts softly, "are you talking about Charlie Marshall's missing million?"

Lenny nodded.

"Who's Charlie Marshall? What Million?" asked Sandra.

"Charlie Marshall nicked a million pounds in 1981. The money was never found."

"We met him in prison," said Taffy.

Sandra stared at her husband. "What were you doing talking to criminals?"

"Who else would we talk to? We were in prison!"

"That's no excuse," said Sandra. "There's criminals and then there's criminals. You were only…"

"It's in a grave in the churchyard," interrupted Lenny, which stopped everyone talking. "You see, his wife had left him, emigrated. He probably wanted to go after her but couldn't get the money. He was a grave digger, so he wouldn't have been earning much," he said, as if explaining things more to himself than anyone else. "Elizabeth, that's his wife, she must have taken all their savings to go herself. So, Charlie, he decides to go back to old ways, and plan a robbery."

"He finds two mugs to help him, and they hold up an armoured car, carrying 1.2 million pounds. But Charlie's not stupid; Charlie knows that the police won't give up easily with that sort of money. So, before they pull the robbery, Charlie orders a headstone and goes to work one last time."

"He digs a grave and hides the headstone in the graveyard. I don't know, perhaps he just covered it with the earth he'd removed. Anyway, the robbery goes ahead. That night Charlie takes the money and gives his mates the slip. He goes to the graveyard, buries it, and puts the headstone in place, keeping a little of the money back. He makes his way to the police station and turns himself, and what he claims to be his share of the money in. Now, the police, anxious to find the rest of the gang and the missing million, start to bargain with Charlie, as he knew they would."

"Charlie cuts a deal for a greatly reduced sentence and turns the rest of the gang in. the rest of the gang is offered a similar deal in return for the missing money, but of course, they don't have the rest of the money. They have nothing to bargain with, so they plead their innocence. The police go back to Charlie, who agrees to give evidence, probably for an even lesser sentence."

"Charlie is a good witness for the prosecution and lays it on thick. After all, it's in his own interest that his mates go to prison for a very long time. Charlie, for all his help, and the only one of the gang to show remorse, is given a five-year sentence and will be free next year to set off to Australia with a million pounds, intending to get back with his wife."

"But something went wrong. His wife met someone else and divorced Charlie. Then, last week, his son David wrote to him, probably to tell him that his mum had remarried."

Lenny thought back. "It upset Charlie; he probably still loves her, and I was there when he got the letter,"

Everyone sat in stunned silence.

"How do you know all this?" asked Taffy.

"Because Elizabeth Ann Marshall is Bill Murphy's sister!"

There was still silence. They hardly dared believe that Lenny could be right.

"Do you know which grave?" asked Sue eventually.

Lenny nodded his head. "That's one mistake he did make; he had his own wife's name put on the headstone.

"Why?" asked Taffy.

"I don't really know why. Perhaps he was still mad at her for leaving him. Although, he did have the words 'My Queen' added at the end. I suppose he loved her and hated her, and he wanted her dead, but then again couldn't bear to give her up... *Never give up your queen."*

A long silence hung over the table before Sue posed the questions, "Wouldn't the police have been interested in this grave?"

"What grave?" said Lenny. "There's no record of a grave, and Charlie wasn't going to mention it to the police, his wife was in Australia. However, once he was in prison he probably became afraid for his wife and son and reverted back to his wife being dead and having no contact with his son story."

"Blimey!" said Jim.

"What are you going to do?" said Janet.

Lenny turned to Numbnuts. "Is that spade still in't car?"

Father Christmas peered over the church wall and witnessed Father O'Connor walking towards the church. He was clearly visible, illuminated by the spotlights, which were set in the floor, lining the path and casting a huge shadow on the church steeple. Father O'Connor unlocked the church doors and went inside.

Lenny knelt back down. "Here's the plan... What's he doing here?"

Lenny was looking at the Grim Reaper, the Virgin Mary, the fairy, the angel, the six-foot penis and the Christmas tree, to Andy Pandy on the end.

"I thought we were going back for a drink," whispered Georgio.

"I invited him back to our house," explained Janet.

"If we're not going back for drinks, what are we doing?"

"We'll explain later," suggested Sandra.

"Right," said Lenny with some frustration, "here's the plan. Somewhere in the churchyard is the grave of Elizabeth Ann

Marshall. I want everyone to split up. If anyone finds the grave, I want you to hoot like an owl, ok?"

"Aye. It's a bit like mission impossible," suggested Numbnuts.

"Shut the fuck up!" suggested Lenny.

The fairy, the angel, the Grim Reaper, the Christmas tree, the six-foot penis, Father Christmas and Andy Pandy climbed over the wall and headed off in different directions.

Father O'Connor finished his prayer, crossed his chest, rose to his feet and left the church locking its great oak doors behind him. The night air was cold, and Father O'Connor did not have a coat, but what he did have was his hip flask. He reached into his pocket and took out the flask. After a quick sip of brandy, he set off back towards his home.

As the old priest rounded the corner, he froze with fear. There, ten feet in front of him, was the Grim Reaper, bending over rubbing the dust from a headstone. Father O'Connor could not believe his eyes.

The Grim Reaper slowly turned and looked at the old priest. There was a long silence, but eventually the reaper spoke from beneath his hood. "Evening."

Father O'Connor could do no more than nod a response, before turning tail and quickly heading back to the church.

Slamming the oak doors behind him, Father O'Connor took out his hip flask and took a longer drink.

Everyone was running tombstone to tombstone.

"I've done that row!" said Lenny in a whispered shout.

"I've done that row," answered Jim.

"Fuck," shouted a voice in the darkness, which sounded like Taffy.

"You found something?" asked Lenny hopefully.

"No," said the voice. "I've fallen over my testicles again!"

Father O'Connor once again crossed his chest and rose from his knees, this time taking a sip of brandy before he left the church. He had eventually convinced himself that it had all been his imagination. 'A hallucination brought on by stress' he told himself.

The angel and the Virgin Mary were standing on the path, bathed in the spotlights that were pointing up at the church spire when suddenly they became aware of another figure on the path. The figure did not move, it just stood perfectly still and stared.

"Evening father," the angel said politely.

The Virgin Mary waved, although hesitantly and with obvious embarrassment.

The old priest clutched his rosary beads and set off back to the church, rapidly repeating a prayer on the way. Inside, Father O'Connor closed the doors behind him. And leaned back on them. The old priest looked up at the ceiling and its impressive 11th century architecture and said another prayer finishing off the contents of his hip flask.

"Not over there!" shouted Numbnuts to Taffy. "I'm sure we were further up the path."

"Jim's looking up the path."

"You go round back then," Numbnuts called as he disappeared into the darkness.

"Fuck this," said Taffy. "I'm going for a fag."

"I just don't think it's right," said Sue as she held up a cigarette lighter to a tombstone, "sneaking around the graveyard in the middle of the night. We'll all end up in prison."

"Oh, be quiet," snapped Sandra, "and pass me that bloody lighter!"

Father O'Connor straightened up his tunic. 'I'm under more stress than I'd thought,' he told himself. 'Perhaps I need a holiday.'

The old priest opened the church doors, and the six-foot penis that was standing in the porch having a cigarette, smiled at him. Father O'Connor let go of the huge brass door handle and the door slowly swung shut in front of him. He leant against the door with his back and passed out.

"Have you found owt?" asked Lenny as he came across Janet in the clearing.

"No, but I've lost one of mi chuffin' wings."

"It dunt matter about your wing, we have to find that gra..." Lenny's words were cut short by the worse owl impression he had ever heard. "Over there," he said setting off in the direction of the sound.

After pushing through some bushes, Lenny came across Georgio standing by a tombstone.

"Was that you?" he asked.

Georgio pointed to the tombstone that read *Elizabeth Ann Marshall. Born 1932. Died 1981. My Queen.*

"Hoot hoot! What the fuck was that?" asked Lenny, although he was really more interested in the tombstone.

"There weren't any owls where I was brought up; I can do a sea eagle."

It wasn't long before Jim arrived. Then Sue, Sandra and Janet arrived together, and were quickly followed by Numbnuts. Lastly, Taffy burst through the bushes, tripping over his testicle as he did so.

Everyone gathered round the grave of Elizabeth Ann Marshall in silence. Lenny took the spade from Jim.

"Are you sure about this?" asked Jim.

"Yeah," said Lenny unconvincingly.

"Sure about what?" asked Georgio.

"Lenny reckons there's a million quid buried in that grave," said Sandra.

Georgio's eyes opened wide. "Fuckin' hell! You're joking?"

Lenny began to dig.

"Are you really sure about this?" asked Sue. "It doesn't seem right, digging up somebody's grave."

"Shut up Sue," commanded Janet. "Does it seem right that we're all on t'poverty line, when there's a million quid buried here doing nowt?"

No one spoke until, five minutes later, Lenny thrust the spade into the earth and then suddenly stopped.

"What is it?" asked Jim.

Lenny didn't answer. He discarded the spade, dropped to his knees and started to brush aside dirt with his bare hands.

"Have you found something?"

"I think so."

Everyone waited with bated breath as Lenny began to pull on a piece of cloth.

Suddenly, the ground around the cloth broke away, and a large hessian sack appeared from the bottom of the hole.

Lenny tossed the sack onto the grass and scrambled out of the hole after it. He tugged at the string trying the neck of the sack until it broke. He looked up at everyone, but somehow, he dared not look inside the sack; he dared not believe he had been right.

"Go on then," said Jim at last.

Lenny slowly reached inside, and just as slowly pulled out a fist full of bank notes.

Within seconds, Jim, Numbnuts, Taffy and Georgio were in the hole tugging at sacks.

Lenny sat on the grass staring at the money and still not quite believing. Within five minutes, ten more sacks had been unearthed.

"Finally," Taffy said, "I think that's it."

"Are you sure?" said Jim.

Numbnuts confirmed that Taffy was right.

Jim picked up two of the sacks. "Right, everyone back to our house."

The sacks were gathered up and everyone set off to Jim's house.

Peter Bellis found a semi-deserted carriage and sat down. The old woman at the far end of the carriage, (the only other occupant), smiled and went back to her magazine. Peter turned and checked the door, and satisfied himself that he was safe.

The experience on the platform had shaken him. He had always been afraid he would be under police surveillance, but he had been desperate to get his hands on his ill-gotten gains. He loosened his kipper tie a little more and sat back in his seat.

What would it have been like if he had been caught with £20,000 of stolen money?

Peter could hardly bear to think about it. For a start, it would have breached his parole condition, which would mean him automatically returning to prison and serving out the remainder of his sentence. That would be three years, plus the charge of handling stolen money!

Peter shuddered to think about it, so he stopped thinking about it. He had gotten away with it, that was all that mattered.

Peter picked up the C&A bag from his side and peered inside, as if to reassure himself that he had gotten away with it. There it was, £20,000 in twenty-pound notes. Peter could almost smell it. He closed the bag and put his head back on the headrest to relax, but far from relaxing his eyes opened wide in a terrified gaze.

In the next car down were two men, one with a raincoat, one wearing a pin-striped suit, and they were coming his way. He recognised them as the same two men he had observed handing about the station. He froze to his seat.

One of the men peered through the glass doors separating the two carriages, and then, to his horror, pointed Peter out to his friend.

Peter jumped up, grabbed the money and ran to the next carriage. He would have kept running if he had not found himself in the very first carriage with the far door firmly shut. Peter turned and watched the two men, who were now in the carriage he had just left and were definitely in pursuit. Peter ran to the window and peered out into the darkness. The carriage lights illuminated bushes and telegraph poles as they zoomed by.

He didn't know what to do, the train was travelling much too fast to jump even if he could have found a door to jump from! He pulled the carrier bag close to his chest as the two men entered his carriage.

"Here he is," said the man in the raincoat. "I told you he'd got on the train. Excuse me, sir."

Peter stood against the window like a frightened animal clutching the bag close to his chest. The two men advanced along the carriage towards him. As they approached, the man in the raincoat reached into his pocket and pulled out his wallet.

Peter opened the window and threw the C&A bag out.

The man stopped for a minute and looked at his friend who shrugged his shoulders.

"We found this wallet," said the man. "It was on the platform where you were standing."

Peter slowly reached out and took the wallet; it was indeed his own. "Thank you."

"That's alright," said the man in the pin-stripe. "Just glad we were getting on the same train. You alright? You look a bit pale."

"Err… yeah. Yes, I'm… I'm fine," said Peter, who did not feel at all fine.

"Well, Happy New Year," said the man in the raincoat.

"Yes, Happy New Year," added his friend.

"Yeah," said Peter.

The Christmas tree, the angel, the Grim Reaper, the Virgin Mary, Andy Pandy, Santa, the six-foot penis and the fairy with the missing wing all burst into Jim's kitchen.

"In here," said Jim, as he put on the living room light,

Everyone threw their sacks down and began to dance; even Taffy and Janet were friends.

"I don't fuckin' believe it," said Taffy, as he flopped back onto the sofa next to Lenny.

"We're rich!" cried Sandra, as she linked arms with Janet and spun around the room.

"I'll get some drinks," said Jim disappearing into the kitchen.

Janet began to sing, *"Who want's to be a millionaire."*

"I do," chorused everyone else.

"Made a bit of a mess," said Sue looking at the mud on the floor.

"Chuff the mess. We'll have the maids clean it up in't morning."

Jim came back in with several bottles and passed them around.

Georgio had been playing with the record player. Music suddenly bellowed out from the twin speakers: *"Money, money, money"*

Everyone joined in: *"It's a rich man's world."*

"I still can't believe it," said Taffy.

"You better believe it," said Jim, grabbing a handful of notes from one of the open bags and throwing them in the air.

"When did you know?" asked Taffy.

"Not until I talked to Bill."

Taffy grabbed Lenny by the cheeks and gave them a squeeze. "Nice one," he said as he got up to dance.

Lenny took a drink from his bottle, before picking up one of the notes that had floated down and settled on his knee. Lenny's smile fell from his face as he gazed at the note. Lenny spent a whole minute gazing at the note in horror, before jumping up and dashing over to the sacks. One after another, he pulled money from each of the sacks, before discarding it and moving onto the next. Eventually, he stopped and sat in silence with his back against the wall. The music was turned off with a scratch of the needle, and everyone looked at Lenny in utter bewilderment.

"What's the matter?" asked Sue quietly.

Lenny held up a fist full of notes from the last bag without speaking.

"What's up with him?" asked Jim.

Taffy approached Lenny and took notes from his hand. Slowly a look of horror came over Taffy too.

Taffy began to look through the discarded notes on the floor.

"What?" asked Jim anxiously.

Taffy scooped up a second lot of notes from the floor and held them up.

"They're all pound notes!"

"So?" said Jim.

Numbnuts scooped up some notes from the floor.

"They're worthless."

"Worthless! What does he mean worthless?" asked Janet.

"He means we can't spend them; they're no longer legal tender," said Taffy slowly.

"We saw it on the news."

"Since when?" asked Jim.

"Since midnight tonight," said Numbnuts.

Jim looked at the clock on the wall; it was nine minutes to midnight.

"So, unless you know a bank manager who will open up his bank in the next nine minutes," continued Numbnuts, "they're worthless"

"That's why there was so much," said Lenny. "Charlie didn't get his decimal point wrong; it was a special delivery. They had just started phasing out the one-pound notes this was a delivery of one-pound notes sent for burning."

Everyone stood in silence.

The minutes on the clock on the wall ticked by.

Lenny screwed up a hand full of notes and threw them on the open fire.

"Why does nothing good ever happen to people like us?" asked Janet as she gazed into the flames.

"Actually," said Numbnuts taking Sandra by the hand, "it does."

There was a long silence.

"You mean?" said Sue.

Sandra was smiling and nodding her head.

"I mean...well," said Numbnuts. "I know it doesn't seem like it, and well, the money's sort of took the edge off it... and we didn't plan on telling you till midnight..."

"What Danny's trying to say is..." Sandra thought for a moment. "Well, I know that money was important, but there are more important things. We're happy; we just wish you could be happy for us."

Everyone looked at each other before Sue spoke. "We are happy for you. Congratulations."

"How? I mean when? I mean when did you find out?" asked Janet.

"I was tested at the clinic this morning."

"That's the best news I've heard all year," said Sue, going over to give Sandra a hug she stealthily slapped her own husband round the back of his head.

Lenny immediately stopped staring at Georgio and held out his hand.

"Nice one, Danny."

"I knew you could do it," said Taffy as he shook Numbnuts' hand while casting a suspicious glance at Georgio.

Although Numbnuts could tell everyone was thoroughly miserable, he appreciated the effort they were all making to at least look happy.

"Well," said Jim, "we may be skint, but we're happy and skint."

"What do you mean we're skint? We're millionaires!" said Taffy, as he looked at the clock. "Well, for the next two minutes anyway!"

"I'll go and get some more drinks," said Jim.

Janet broke off embracing Sandra. "I'll get the sandwiches."

Janet and Jim went into the kitchen, leaving everyone either hugging or shaking hands.

"You know what?" said Jim as he began to open the first of several bottles of lager.

"What?"

"I wouldn't mind trying for another kid."

"You've had the snip you daft chuff!" said Janet, as she leaned over to retrieve the sandwiches from the fridge.

"Still, dunt stop us trying though, does it?"

Janet felt her bottom being pinched and her face lit up brighter than the interior of her fridge.

"Drinks anyone?" said Jim as he entered into the room.

"Yeah, I'll have one."

"Lovely."

"Me too."

"And me."

"Pass one here."

"Don't mind if I do."

"Cucumber sandwiches anyone?" asked Janet.

"Not for me thanks."

"I'm not bothered."

"No… thanks."

"I'm dieting."

"No ta."

"I'm not hungry."

Janet looked at Sue who was looking sheepish, as indeed was everyone else.

Suddenly, the clock began to chime.

"Come on everybody," said Sandra, as she crossed her arms and took her husband's hand.

Everyone shuffled around until they formed a circle. As they linked arms began to sing.

'Should auld acquaintance be forgot and never brought to mind'

"You know," said Lenny to Numbnuts, "I quite enjoyed being a millionaire. It beats having nowt by a million."

"Should auld acquaintance be forgot..."

Numbnuts smiled as he looked around the room. "We'll never have nowt. Anyway, I still feel like a millionaire!"

"For the sake of auld lang syne."

Colin Vine turned his collar up against the rain. The moon had disappeared behind a cloud and Colin was beginning to have doubts. 'Perhaps there were no trains at night,' he told himself. Perhaps if he stayed here much longer, he would die of hypothermia.

Just as he was about to give up Colin noticed a light in the distance. He waited and the light drew closer. 'This is for the best,' he told himself. 'Mum's going to be alright'.

The light drew closer, and Colin could now see other lights following it, as the train rounded the corner and headed straight towards him. He had checked on his insurance and it was paid up, one of the few things that were. "This will all be over in a second' he told himself.

The train thundered along the track; its light now close enough to illuminate the ground around him. Colin looked down at the rails running either side of him. 'It will all be over in a moment'.

The train lines grew brighter and the sleeper beneath his feet started to vibrate. Colin looked up, the train was almost on him, and he closed his eyes. The inside of his eyelids grew brighter and brighter and, for the first time he could hear the engine.

'This is it!' he told himself as he tensed every muscle in his body.

Suddenly, Colin felt an impact that knocked him onto his back. His chest hurt and the wind had been knocked out of him, but there was something wrong: He wasn't dead.

Colin quickly ascertained that the train that had been hurtling towards him was now passing him by. He opened his eyes to the realisation that he had been standing on a duel tracked section of the railway line – on the wrong track! But then, what had hit him in the chest? What had knocked him on his back? Colin sat up, in his lap was a carrier bag labelled 'C&A'. The carrier bag had been ripped open by the impact, and lying all around were bundles and bundles of twenty-pound notes.

Epilogue

1990

Lenny sat at the picnic bench by the boating lake, and waved to Colin as he pushed his mother along in her wheelchair. It was a beautiful afternoon and Lenny was enjoying it, having just completed his day shift at the mine, (which had so far survived the pit closure plan).

"Sorry I'm late," said Sue as she approached. "Tommy O'Brien and Martin Shaw have been fighting again, and I had to give them detention."

Sue sat down and piled a handful of exercise books on the table. "Where are Danny and Sandra?"

Lenny pointed to the lake. "Over there, they've taken the boys out on the boat."

Sue looked out onto the lake and saw Danny, (who hadn't been called Numbnuts for the last six years) and Sandra rowing a boat. In the back sat the twins, Daniel Jr. and little Leonard, their bright red hair glistening in the sunlight.

Sue opened one of the exercise books.

"What are you doing?" asked Lenny.

"Marking homework."

Lenny thought for a moment. "Dunt seem two minutes since we were doing homework. Can you remember?"

"Yeah, you were always good at stories. Used to fancy yourself as a writer."

"Used to fancy you, you mean!" Sue slid an exercise book across the table. "Here, write me a story."

Lenny laughed. "Ok. What's the subject?"

Sue picked up one of the books. "Do you know, I can't remember... Oh yes... *A time I'll always remember."*

Lenny smiled, picked up a pen, and began to write.

Everyone always said things would get worse before they got better. The trouble was no one said how bad worse was going to be.

Someone once said: "When you've got nothing you've got nothing to lose." Well. I suppose that's how we saw it at the time.

We were wrong; we had each other, and that was all we needed.

On the 3rd of March 1985, the National Executive of the NUM voted for a return to work.

There were 170 mines employing over 191,700 men.

On the 18th of December 2015 Kellingley Colliery closed... It was the last coal mine in the UK.